Rich...

He had ...
come to like her quite a ...
Phoebe had stood up to her sister at the rally,
and he'd enjoyed going over to her house and
seeing how she lived.

What also was making him look at her a little
differently was the way her body felt pressed
up against him. He knew he had no right at all
to be thinking about his boss's body, although
he was human, wasn't he? But he just
couldn't help it. The thing was, they fit well
together.

It had something to do with her height.
Instead of her head being way down below his
chest somewhere, it was right up against his,
and he had this big urge to turn his face a few
degrees so that he could kiss her....

ABOUT THE AUTHOR

The only thing Beverly Sommers likes to do more than write romances is to travel. And, of course, reading spy novels. And watching football. Or even basketball. In fact, any sport. And then there's shopping, talking on the phone, going to the movies, relaxing on the beach, writing letters, eating Chinese food, listening to Huey Lewis and the News, visiting friends, even going for walks. When she's not doing any of these things, she's usually writing.

Books by Beverly Sommers

HARLEQUIN AMERICAN ROMANCE

11–CITY LIFE, CITY LOVE
26–UNSCHEDULED LOVE
62–VERDICT OF LOVE
69–THE LAST KEY
85–MIX AND MATCH
125–CHANGING PLACES
137–CONVICTIONS
152–SNOWBIRD
165–LE CLUB
179–SILENT NIGHT

HARLEQUIN INTRIGUE

3–MISTAKEN IDENTITY

Don't miss any of our special offers. Write to us at the following address for information on our newest releases.

Harlequin Reader Service
901 Fuhrmann Blvd., P.O. Box 1397, Buffalo, NY 14240
Canadian address: P.O. Box 603,
Fort Erie, Ont. L2A 5X3

Phoebe's Deputy
Beverly Sommers

Harlequin Books

TORONTO • NEW YORK • LONDON
AMSTERDAM • PARIS • SYDNEY • HAMBURG
STOCKHOLM • ATHENS • TOKYO • MILAN

Published March 1987

First printing January 1987

ISBN 0-373-16191-3

Copyright © 1987 by Beverly Sommers. All rights reserved.
Philippine copyright 1987. Australian copyright 1987.
Except for use in any review, the reproduction or utilization of
this work in whole or in part in any form by any electronic,
mechanical or other means, now known or hereafter invented,
including xerography, photocopying and recording, or in any
information storage or retrieval system, is forbidden without
the permission of the publisher, Harlequin Enterprises Limited,
225 Duncan Mill Road, Don Mills, Ontario, Canada M3B 3K9.

All the characters in this book have no existence outside the
imagination of the author and have no relation whatsoever to
anyone bearing the same name or names. They are not even
distantly inspired by any individual known or unknown to the
author, and all incidents are pure invention.

The Harlequin trademarks, consisting of the words
HARLEQUIN AMERICAN ROMANCE, HARLEQUIN
AMERICAN ROMANCES, and the portrayal of a Harlequin,
are trademarks of Harlequin Enterprises Limited; the portrayal
of a Harlequin is registered in the United States Patent and
Trademark Office and in the Canada Trade Marks Office.

Printed in Canada

Chapter One

In a sheltered nook by a bend in the road, Phoebe Tripp lived alone with her children. Her small house, nestled against the mountain, was jerry-built and badly in need of paint. The rest of the nook was occupied by a vegetable patch, a chicken coop and a VW bug, all currently covered by snow.

There were no telephone lines in the vicinity; the tin roof did not display a television antenna. The nearest town, Greensboro Bend, was eleven miles up the road. If you could call Greensboro Bend a town. A real estate agent with unusual self-control might describe it as a village.

Phoebe, who had lived most of her life in Princeton, New Jersey, considered herself a survivalist after living a year and a half in Greensboro Bend.

Phoebe the survivalist had just survived another tightly compressed fifteen minutes, the time it took her, on a good morning, to see Ben and Dory off to school. She had it down to a science. Bowls containing individual boxes of cereal were set out on the table the night before. A week's worth of lunches were made every Sunday and then frozen. A morning bathroom schedule was posted. The children were old enough to pick out their own clothes and dress themselves.

Phoebe liked things organized. Without organization, she felt that the world, or at least her world, was likely to collapse inward on itself. To forestall this implosion, she made constant lists, left trails of memos to her children—sometimes held by fruit-shaped magnets to the refrigerator, sometimes left on pillows. She planned everything, fearing, if she didn't, that it would be left to her to improvise, and Phoebe had never been good at improvisation.

This particular morning, no sooner had she waved her children off on their mile hike to catch the school bus, no sooner had she collapsed in the nearest chair to finish her cup of black coffee and her first Salem of the day, no sooner had she opted in favor of going back to bed for another hour or two and trying—without success, she knew—to revive the rather animated dream she had been having, than there came a rapping upon her door. The rapping struck her as ominous.

Her first inclination was to ignore it, but without phone service, house calls were the only way anyone could reach her. On the other hand, there was no one she particularly wanted to see at the moment. Still, the few people she knew were also familiar with her sleeping habits, which meant it must be important for someone to get over to her place at the ungodly hour of eight-twenty in the morning.

While she was still debating whether to get up and answer the door, the rapping came again. Louder this time. More like pounding than rapping. She felt pounding was rude, but had to admit it sounded more urgent.

Phoebe's Deputy

Phoebe, a large flannel shirt over her ex-husband's pajamas, her feet in fuzzy slippers that were made to resemble armadillos, her hair sticking out every which way, reluctantly set aside her coffee, put out her cigarette and shuffled to the door.

This was Vermont, so there weren't ten locks on the door. This was rural Vermont, so there was one strong lock and a chain, just in case. She unlocked the lock, left the chain on and opened the door four inches.

Prince Charming always arrives at the wrong time. There he stood, big as life. And blurred. Without her glasses, any man looked like Prince Charming to Phoebe. Which added a little romance to life, in her opinion. Forget that once she put on her glasses he would likely turn into a frog. The few men she had so far come into contact with in Vermont had all seemed to resemble frogs, a fact that she attributed to the weather. For that matter, with her myopia, she supposed it could be a large woman standing there.

The fuzzy image spoke, and it was definitely a male voice. A rural voice, which meant ten beats slower than Phoebe's.

"I'm trying to locate Phoebe Tripp, ma'am."

Instantly recognizing the sound of authority, she felt herself become tense. "Why?" she asked.

"Official business, ma'am."

Paranoia time. "Official?"

She saw some blurred movement, then he was holding something out to her that caught the reflection of the scant amount of sunshine on the usual overcast March day.

"Orleans County Sheriff's Department, ma'am."

And, being a law-abiding citizen, Phoebe immediately felt guilty. The reason for his being there didn't dawn on her, which she later attributed to it being too early in the morning for rational thinking.

"What is it you want exactly?" she asked him, knowing damn well her skin was already blushing the way it always did when she felt guilty about something. Blushing in the way she would have been blushing if she had had a pound of marijuana hidden in her closet or assault rifles stashed in her chicken coop. All her life she had been accused of things she hadn't done simply because her blush made her look guilty.

"Could I come in for a moment?" he wanted to know.

Along with her blush, her stomach began to tighten. "I think not," said Phoebe, wondering if she should ask him whether he had a search warrant or, perhaps, just throw herself on his mercy.

There was the sound of a throat being cleared, and she knew that when he spoke it was going to be bad news for her. "It's the election, ma'am. You're the new sheriff."

It took ten seconds for the words to sink in. Then, "Impossible," said Phoebe, slamming the door in his face. She stood there in shock. A joke, that's what it was. A practical joke no doubt set up by her sister. Mavis possessed a weird sense of humor. She always had, even as a child.

Phoebe returned to her cup of coffee and downed it as though it were a shot of whiskey. The effect, however, was not the same. Cold coffee does little to lessen the effects of shock.

A gentle tapping started again on the door. She wondered if he'd keep tapping while she got dressed, combed her hair, found her glasses and put on a little makeup. When the tapping quickly turned into pounding, she decided not.

Opening the door once again, this time showing him only one eye and part of her forehead, she said, "I know this must be some kind of a joke. My sister, Mavis, sent you over here, right?"

"It's no joke, ma'am. If it's any consolation, no one I've talked to is any happier about it than you are."

An understatement. Definitely an understatement. "It's hard to believe that the first time in my life I've ever won anything, it had to be sheriff. Why couldn't it have been a lottery?"

"I'm sorry, ma'am."

His steadfast politeness was beginning to get on her nerves. "My running against the sheriff was just a gesture," she tried to explain. "I wasn't supposed to win. Anyway, how could I possibly have won? I've heard Sheriff Benson hasn't lost an election in twenty-five years."

"It was a technicality," said the man, who no doubt was a deputy, and she thought she heard a smile in his voice. "The vote was overwhelmingly in his favor, but we found out this morning that he had neglected to file. Which, legally, makes you the new sheriff of Orleans County. May I be the first to congratulate you?"

Congratulations weren't what she was looking for. What she was looking for was a way out. "Isn't he going to fight it?" Phoebe asked.

"I'm sure that will occur to him as soon as he sobers up. In the meantime, I'm to escort you to the county clerk's office so you can get sworn in."

She supposed she would have to go with him. If she refused, he might be capable of dragging her down there without even giving her time to get dressed. With real regret she thought of the sleep she was going to miss. "I'll need twenty minutes to get ready," she told him, knowing she'd need at least thirty.

"I'll be waiting in the car for you, ma'am."

THIS WAS ALL THANKS to Mavis; Mavis and her Crazy Quilt Women's Commune—the same commune Phoebe and her kids had lived in briefly while house hunting for something she could afford.

It was the kind of commune that women appeared to use as a halfway house. Divorced women would live there temporarily while they got their lives back in order. Women just out of college who were used to dormitory living would avail themselves of the commune until they found jobs and moved elsewhere. Occasionally an evicted woman or a battered wife would be given a room. Lonely women sometimes found it a friendly refuge. And then there was Mavis, her sister, who actually thought of it as an alternative way of life and believed that all women would be better off living in a women's commune.

Phoebe should have said no immediately when Mavis had asked her if she'd be willing to run on the ballot against Sheriff Benson. Actually, she had said no, but she should have stuck with it. Mavis, however, could be persuasive.

"It isn't as though you'll win," Mavis had assured her. "It's just that we don't have much of a democratic process when no one ever runs against Billy Benson. And we think it's time for a female to run for sheriff in this county."

Phoebe had never given much thought to democratic processes and didn't want to begin doing so. "Run yourself" had been Phoebe's advice.

"I would," said Mavis, "but a lot of the people around here think our commune is a joke. I would lack credibility."

"Get Mom to run."

"Mom's not into social responsibility these days."

"Listen, Mavis, you know as well as I do that I'd be no good at making speeches and campaigning. I'm not even any good at talking on the phone," she added, wishing her sister would get off her back, but knowing she owed her, too.

"Nobody ever campaigns for the job. Anyway, you owe me," said Mavis.

Phoebe had been hoping she wouldn't bring that up. "I'm not even a real Vermonter. Aren't there some kind of requirements for the job?"

"You're a resident," said Mavis, "which is all that's required. Plus you're old enough, of course."

Phoebe felt herself backing down, the way she always ended up backing down when Mavis wanted something from her. And she couldn't help thinking that maybe she was overreacting to a very minor favor this time, one that would get her out of Mavis's debt. It wasn't as though she'd be a serious candidate. No one was likely to actually vote for her. "Under one condition," she stipulated.

"You've got it." Mavis's jubilation was barely checked.

"The condition is, none of you can vote for me. I don't want some freak election where no one turns out to vote because they figure the sheriff is a shoo-in." That request seemed safe enough, since she hardly knew anyone in Greensboro Bend.

"That's a tough condition," said Mavis.

"You don't have to vote for the sheriff—just don't vote for me. That's it. Take it or leave it."

After some hesitation on Mavis's part, they shook on it.

That should teach Phoebe never to get into anyone's debt again. However, without Mavis's intervention, Phoebe, in the shocked state she had been in when Ted had told her he wanted a divorce so he could marry one of his graduate students, would have been lost. One call to Mavis, though, and Mavis had flown to Princeton, New Jersey, hired Phoebe a feminist divorce lawyer, and instead of getting nothing, Phoebe had wound up with a small settlement, which had gone into purchasing the house she was living in, and four hundred dollars a month in child support. That amount supported all three of them—not in style, of course, but Phoebe was willing to forgo style in order to be able to stay home with Ben and Dory.

She wondered why Mavis hadn't driven by first thing to break the glad tidings. Surely the commune, with their shortwave radio and Sony Trinitron, had been up on the election results. Not that she would blame Mavis if she heretofore tried to avoid her. Mavis must know what would be going through her sister's mind. Mavis probably feared for her life. With good reason.

Sheriff? It was like waking up from a bad dream and finding out it was reality.

THIRTY MINUTES LATER and five pounds of clothing heavier, Phoebe, her wiry red curls subdued beneath a navy watch cap, her wire-rimmed spectacles in place, her lips a healthy shade of pink, her colorless eyelashes now Maybelline's brownish black, climbed into the sheriff's department sedan and got her first focused look at her early morning caller.

Prince Charming he was not. On the plus side, though, he didn't at all resemble a frog. The fact of the matter was, the deputy rather resembled an Indian of the American variety. Thick, straight black hair fell over his forehead; eyes as brownish black as her mascara inspected her; a roughly chiseled mouth tightened; and a large, straight nose and high cheekbones completed the picture. The only thing lacking was dark skin and a loincloth, but she was sure there was Indian blood in his background somewhere.

"I'm Deputy Stuart, ma'am."

Phoebe was disappointed. She had been hoping his name would be something like Snake Eyes. Or Howling Wolf. Maybe Swift Hawk in Flight. "Please don't keep calling me 'ma'am,'" she told him, sure he wasn't a day younger than she was. It was even possible he was slightly older.

This brought the beginnings of a smile to his face, brightening it considerably and making him look less like an Indian. "You can call me 'Richie.'"

"Just call me 'Sheriff,'" she said, making what she thought was a joke, then realized he had taken it the wrong way when his smile vanished without a trace. He started the engine and roared down the road, only the fact that it was covered with snow preventing him from burning rubber. Very childish behavior, in her view. He obviously didn't like calling her "Sheriff," which was the same as calling her "Boss."

She felt like saying, "Come on, quit acting like a kid," which is something she often said to her own kids, who always reacted by saying, "But we *are* kids, Mom." It would sound condescending, though, not at all the kind of thing she should say to this sheriff's deputy. She had a feeling she hadn't made much of an impression on him up to now, even without the "call me Sheriff" remark, and she better make some kind of amends fast, because now he was sitting there in the driver's seat, looking like a wooden Indian.

"I was just joking, Richie," she said, looking out the window as she said it.

"Joking?"

"You know, when I said to call me 'Sheriff.'"

"No need to apologize."

"I wasn't apologizing," said Phoebe, suddenly feeling on the defensive. "This whole situation seems like a joke, so I was just joking around. For heaven's sake, call me 'Phoebe.'"

"I'd just as soon call you 'Sheriff.'"

"I've always had this thing about my name," said Phoebe, wondering why she wasn't able to keep her mouth shut. Silences bothered her, though; they always had. Luckily, with two kids around, she didn't have to suffer them often. "Phoebe. It sounds so silly, that name. I never thought it suited me. When I was little I couldn't pronounce it and it came out sounding like 'Fifi,' and my parents thought that was cute and called me 'Fifi' until I started school and put an end to it. I'd be somewhere with my mother, like the grocery store, and my mother would call out, 'Come here, Fifi,' and everyone would look around for a French poodle."

The first crack in the wooden face appeared when she saw the movement around his mouth. If she wasn't mistaken, he was trying not to laugh. "Why couldn't she just have named me something normal, like Debby or Cindi? Nobody my age is named Phoebe. It makes me sound like an anachronism."

His face had begun to lose its tight look as his hands unclenched from the steering wheel. Unlike some people in her family—notably Mavis—she didn't mind poking fun at herself to lighten up a situation. He was looking almost human now. "Like your name," she said, not thinking much about what she was saying, just going with it since it seemed to be working. "I wouldn't have figured you for a Richie. Lone Wolf, maybe, or Running Ocelot."

"Come again?" he said, his tones sounding strangled.

"What I mean is an Indian name," said Phoebe. "Richie sounds too...I don't know, too boyish, I guess. Too all-American."

"An Indian name?" He was looking at her now in a way that suggested he was examining a new species of insect.

"Well, you are Indian, aren't you? I mean, you sure look it."

"No, I'm not."

"You're not? Are you sure?"

"I'm not an Indian, Sheriff. I was named Richard after my father."

"Someone must have told you you looked like an Indian before. I couldn't be the first."

"You're the first."

Feeling really stupid now, Phoebe changed the subject. "Do I really have to get sworn in? Surely everything will be straightened out eventually and Sheriff Benson will be back at work."

The change of subject appeared to be too fast for him as he took a little time to answer. "Maybe, but in the interim we need a sheriff."

"Perhaps I'll appoint you sheriff," she said, thinking that would be an easy way to get out of it. And he certainly looked more like a sheriff than she did. Well, maybe not exactly like a sheriff. In Westerns sheriffs were never Indians.

"You can't appoint me. It's an elected office."

"Then why didn't you run? How come I had to get stuck with it?"

"If you didn't want it, why did you put your name on the ballot?"

"I was assured I wouldn't win. It was just supposed to be a gesture. A protest. A stupid idea my sister's commune had and that she, unfortunately, talked me into."

He turned to give her a quick look. "That group of crazy ladies on that farm?"

"Not crazy ladies. It's called the Crazy Quilt Women's Commune."

"They seem crazy to me," said Richie.

Phoebe didn't argue the point. In many ways her sister's group did act a little crazy. Like those ridiculous clothes they dressed up in whenever there was a full moon. Like refusing to have roosters on their farm even though it meant they wouldn't get the next generation of chickens. Like making her run for sheriff.

"How many deputies are there?" she asked him.

"Let's just say if we got hit by a train now, the entire sheriff's department would be wiped out."

"It's just you and me?"

"That's about the size of it, Sheriff."

"For the entire county?"

Phoebe's Deputy   17

"It's not a well-populated area. Mostly all we do is execute court orders and keep the peace. Sometimes we transport prisoners, but not often."

"Aren't there shifts or anything? Are we on call twenty-four hours a day, seven days a week?" If so, it was something she was going to have to get out of fast.

"Why didn't you find out this stuff before you got into it?"

"I told you—I didn't plan on being elected."

"Well, don't worry about it. We work nine to five, five days a week. The rest of the time the state police take over."

For a nine-to-five job, it didn't sound as bad as she had thought. She pictured herself sitting in an office, answering the phone and sending Richie out to keep the peace. She thought it could've been a lot worse.

Then, like a news flash that interrupts a regularly scheduled broadcast, Phoebe was hit with a memory. She couldn't remember who told her, but it must have been Mavis. She relied on Mavis for all her news. Their mother, the redoubtable Katie Lou, was keeping company with a law enforcement person, and if she had been told a name, it escaped her.

She stole a glance at Richie. She didn't even know him and it was always difficult to like the bearer of bad news. Indeed, there had been civilizations that had killed the bearers of bad news, and coming to her house to tell her she had been elected sheriff had definitely been bearing bad news. It was also bad news, though, that her mother could attract such a man, when she was practically positive that she herself wouldn't be capable of getting to first base with him—if he was the law enforcement person in question. And that was a distinct possibility. But even if he wasn't the one, she was sure her mother could attract him.

But, then, her mother wasn't lanky and covered with freckles; her mother was Greensboro Bend's answer to Joan Collins. With a little help from the cosmetic manufacturers of the world, of course.

She sneaked another look at him, wondering if she would even want to get to first base with him. On looks alone, yes. On personality, just maybe. He appeared to have little sense of humor, or he would be joking about her election. She kept hoping he would. Because he didn't, she was being forced to view it more seriously than she would like.

Getting a job had occurred to her from time to time, usually when the bills arrived. And if she had wanted a job and had set out to get one, she didn't think she would've been successful. First of all, there weren't any jobs in Greensboro Bend, and second of all, even if there were, she didn't think she'd qualify. About all she was qualified to do was baby-sit, and the teenage girls were practically killing one another for those jobs.

If someone had said to Phoebe, "Would you like to have your own office and a man to do the work for you?" she would have been tempted to apply for the job. She would have wanted to know about it in advance, though, so she could prepare for it. The news that she had gotten the job of sheriff had come too suddenly. She hated surprises. Her husband's leaving her had been the biggest surprise in her life, and she still hadn't recovered from it.

Being elected sheriff was definitely the second biggest. And another one that she wasn't prepared for.

Being unprepared for a surprise was on a par with being caught downtown in her underwear. Both were untenable.

In fact, she didn't even want to think about it. "Are we almost there?" she asked him.

"You don't know?"

"I'm not asking just to make conversation," she said, then realized how rude she sounded. But sometimes when she was scared she got rude. She didn't know why that was, but it had happened before.

His mouth tightened. "Yes, we're almost there. I guess I just naturally assumed, since you were running for sheriff, that you knew where you'd be working in the eventuality that you won."

With Richie, she was thinking, a little sarcasm went a long way. But, then, she shouldn't have started it. She decided she'd better shut up the rest of the trip.

She began to wonder if he was her mother's type. That was a waste of time, because of course he was her mother's type. He was a good-looking young man, wasn't he? Only that wasn't really being fair. After being married to a man twenty years older than her, why shouldn't her mother enjoy herself now that she was a widow?

Poor Dad had never known what he'd missed. Not six months after his death, the subdued faculty wife had turned into the femme fatale of Greensboro Bend. Instead of quietly slipping into a life of good deeds in Princeton, New Jersey, her mother had moved permanently to the house on the lake in Vermont where they had always spent their summer vacations. Not to retire, though, but to buy one of the local taverns.

It was strange the way they had all ended up in Greensboro Bend. First her mother had moved there, then Mavis had decided to drop out of the academic world and start a commune there. Phoebe had always loved spending summers there, where it was cool while New Jersey was steaming, but she had never pictured herself moving to a place where it snowed most of the year. But, then, Mavis had been persuasive that time, too, and Phoebe hadn't wanted to stay in Princeton, where she would be sure to run into Ted and his new wife. Plus she had missed her mother, but it had been the old mother she had missed, not the new one Katie Lou had become in Greensboro Bend.

Was she jealous of her mother? Probably. Phoebe had never been the femme fatale of anything. She had never even had a date in high school. It wasn't that she looked that bad; it was more that she was so shy in those days that she blushed if a boy even looked in her direction.

Just as she blushed now, when she saw that Richie was looking at her. "We're here," he said, and she belatedly noticed he had stopped in front of the electric building in town. "Why don't you get out and I'll park around the corner?"

"This is where I pay my electric bill," said Phoebe, looking out at the old, stone building.

"It also houses the city clerk and the sheriff's department."

Phoebe, feeling very much as though she were on her way to her own execution, got out of the car. She took care not to slam the door, walked carefully along the shoveled sidewalk; then, as she stepped up onto the stoop, she skidded on the ice and fell down hard.

"Oh, dear," she thought aloud, "I can see the headline now—'New Sheriff Falls Flat on Her A _ _ !'"

Phoebe's Deputy

RICHIE, ALTHOUGH HE WOULD HAVE undergone torture before admitting it, had voted for Phoebe Tripp. Not as a tribute to her, however. More as a protest against the existing sheriff, old rotgut Billy Benson himself. Billy was neither efficient, diligent nor a pleasure to work for. His attitudes were antiquated. To him, any kid with hair longer than a crew cut was a drug dealer. Currently popular music was un-American if not a communist plot. Being gay was sacrilegious. Plus he believed book learning was suspect and payoffs, in the form of favors, were part of correct police procedure.

A female sheriff, though, might be trading in one problem for another. Richie would have given her the benefit of the doubt, but not after he heard the election had been a joke to her. Some plot by that crazy female commune just to make a statement. He took police work too seriously to stand for that kind of attitude.

Maybe he should have run himself. It would have meant his job, of course, and who was to know old Billy would neglect to file? Although it might have been that if he had really campaigned against Billy, the rest of the populace, who were as tired of Sheriff Benson's policies as he was, might have elected him.

Phoebe Tripp. Was she for real? Was she aware she was about to be sworn in wearing the strangest-looking bedroom slippers he had ever seen, or was she as eccentric as she appeared to be?

He couldn't wait for Daryl, the city clerk, to get a load of her looks and the nonsense that spouted from her mouth. Not that she was naturally ugly; by no means was she that. It was just that she'd take the blue ribbon at any county fair for the most successful attempt by a decent-looking woman to make herself as unappealing as possible. He was sure glad he had Maggie so he wouldn't even be tempted by Sheriff Phoebe "Call Me 'Sheriff'" Tripp.

He entered the building through a side door and walked down the corridor to the office of the city clerk. When he got there, Tracy, the clerk typist, was at the typewriter, no doubt composing poems rather than doing official work, and Daryl was sitting with his feet up on his desk, a bag from the local doughnut place brushing against his shoes. Business as usual in the busy metropolis of Greensboro Bend.

"Where is she?" Richie asked them.

"I'm here," answered Tracy, looking up from her typewriter.

"I was referring to our new sheriff."

"I thought you went to get her," Daryl said.

"I did," Richie said, backing out of the office and going down the hall to the front door of the building. And there she was, standing out in the cold like a bedraggled cat waiting to be let in the house. The tall redhead with the big mouth couldn't be shy, could she?

"Come on in," he told her. "You don't have to wait to be invited."

She gave him a hesitant look, then followed him down the hall. Total silence greeted her arrival.

He gestured toward the others. "That's Tracy at the typewriter and Daryl, our city clerk, looking comfortable." Daryl immediately took his feet off the desk and tried to look official. The try failed miserably.

"This is the new sheriff, guys," said Richie. "She's not informal, like Billy—she prefers being addressed as 'Sheriff.'"

He took a quick look at her and saw she was blushing. Again. He didn't quite know what to make of it. Either she was shyer than she seemed or she was into having hot flashes. But she looked a little young to be having hot flashes.

Daryl said, "Pleasure meeting you," and Tracy didn't say anything. She appeared to be mesmerized by the slippers on the new sheriff's feet.

"Are those armadillos? I just love them," she said.

Sheriff Tripp turned from a pleasing shade of pink to a rather mottled red. Richie watched as she glanced slowly downward until her eyes zeroed in on her feet.

"Why didn't you tell me?" she said, looking straight at Richie.

"Tell you what, Sheriff?" he asked, acting as though he thought there was nothing unusual about her footgear.

The sheriff turned a beleaguered look in Tracy's direction. "Thank you, I love them, too. It's just that I don't normally wear them out of the house. This morning, though, wasn't like any other morning. I'm afraid I didn't expect to be elected sheriff."

"I know just what you mean," Tracy said, then got the kind of look on her face that told Richie she had thought up a new idea for a poem. He was sure that armadillos would appear in it somewhere.

Before she went totally off into her own world of poetic endeavor, though, Tracy said, "We're all ready here to swear you in. Whenever you're ready, of course."

"Thanks," said Phoebe. "I'll just get out of this stuff." Then the sheriff began discarding her outer garments, while they all looked on with interest.

Off came the surplus paratrooper's parka. Off came the hunter's vest in bright orange and the black-and-red lumberjack's shirt. What remained was a turtleneck sweater and narrow-legged jeans. What had started out as the shape of a polar bear, gradually, layer by layer, began to assume the slim form of a fashion model. Or maybe Richie was being generous. Maybe skinny was the correct word. She was skinny, but all the parts were where they belonged.

Last of all, off came the watch cap and out sprang a mop—and "mop" was the precise word—of unruly orange hair. He had gotten a glimpse of it through the door, but seeing all of it at one time was something of a shock. He figured she had enough hair to cover a dozen bald heads with some left over.

And of course the armadillos remained.

Richie heard a sigh coming from Daryl's direction and knew that sheriff or no sheriff, Daryl would give it his best try. There weren't many single women in Greensboro Bend, and Daryl gave them all his best try.

Daryl got to his feet and tried on his official look again. "This is the first time I've ever sworn in a sheriff," he said, "so bear with me. If you'll just raise your right hand..."

And then he was off and running, sounding rather like one of those auctioneers they got in for the summer antique sales. The ceremony went by Richie so fast he couldn't understand a word of it, and judging from Phoebe's expression, she wasn't faring any better. At the end of it, though, it looked as though they had gotten themselves a new sheriff.

And it just could be, Richie was thinking, that her first act in office might be to fire him.

And the thing was, if she didn't fire him, was he going to be able to take orders from a woman?

Chapter Two

Ben let himself in the front door with his own key. His other hand was clutching his bulging jacket. Once inside, he unzipped the jacket and a large, black cat instantly escaped and went tearing up the wooden steps to the loft. Which, Ben thought, was a good move on the cat's part.

He didn't see his mom in the living room and there was no light on in the kitchen, so he went into the bathroom and out the other side, where his mother's bedroom was. There had been times when he had gotten home from school and found his mother still in bed. She called it a nap, but Dory called it sleeping all day. He didn't mind, because as soon as he would get home she would get up to be with him, and a lot of the time she looked really tired, as though she didn't get enough sleep.

Dory thought everyone got too much sleep. Dory thought sleeping was a waste of time and did as little of it as possible, sometimes reading in bed at night with a flashlight.

Today, however, his mother's bed was unmade but empty. "Mom?" he called out in a tentative voice. When there was no answer, he went into the kitchen, turned on the light and got himself a glass of orange juice out of the refrigerator. It had never happened before that he had come home from school and not found his mom there. Maybe that meant that what he had heard in school was really true.

He hadn't really believed it because his mom had said it would never happen, and even if he had, he wouldn't have realized it might mean that his mother wouldn't be in the house anymore when he got home. He didn't like that much. Except that now he could eat as many cookies as he wanted, making sure, though, to leave a few for Dory when she got home. Because if he didn't, Dory would be mean to him.

Not that she would be mean to him in a way that would hurt him. She wouldn't hit him or pinch him or anything like that. She would just say things to him that would make him feel like a baby. She did that sometimes when his mother wasn't around, and sometimes even when she was around, but then his mom would tell Dory to cut it out.

Eight wasn't a baby at all. Still, he wished his mother were at home.

When Dory arrived a half-hour later, the cat was still hiding in the loft and Ben had eaten all the cookies but two. He figured two were enough for her. Dory was fat. "Stocky" was what his mom called it, but Dory herself said she was getting fat and always said it in a proud way.

Dory walked in, slammed the door, then looked around at all the lights on. "Where's Mom?" she asked him.

"Dunno. She wasn't home."

Dory gave a smug nod. "Just as I suspected. And she made believe it was all a big joke."

"It's really true?" asked Ben.

"Sure looks that way," said Dory. "We haven't got a mother anymore, Ben. We have the law living in the house with us."

"What is a sheriff, Dory? It's like a policeman, isn't it?"

"Precisely."

Ben thought about that for a moment. "You mean like that Dirty Harry movie I watched over at Jason's house that Mom said was too violent for me to watch?"

"Just call Mom Clint Eastwood from now on."

"Why?"

"Just a joke, Ben. He's the actor who played in the movie."

"Oh. I thought Dirty Harry was a real person. Will Mom have a gun, Dory?"

"I would imagine so."

Ben began to smile. If he carried a real gun to school he would be sure to be chosen first to be on teams. He might even get to do the choosing. "And will she shoot all the bad people?"

"I don't think there are any bad people around here, Ben. This is a pretty quiet place."

"Then why does Mom always tell me not to talk to strangers?"

"Just in case."

Dory settled down on the couch, and as she did so, Ben noticed her eyes widen. He followed their gaze and saw the cat peering down between the wooden rails that enclosed the loft.

"Another cat follow you home?" asked Dory.

"I couldn't help it," said Ben. "I couldn't get rid of him and he looked so cold and hungry." Ben knew it was a lie and didn't like telling lies, but when it came to cats he felt he had to.

"He looks pretty well fed to me. Is he wearing a collar?"

"No," said Ben, who had taken off the collar and stuffed it inside his book bag.

"You realize, Ben, that if that cat belongs to someone, it's stealing, and Mom will have to lock you up in jail."

Ben didn't believe his mom would ever lock him up in jail, not even if he did something really bad. "I didn't steal him—he was outside. It's like finding money on the road. It's not stealing if you pick it up and keep it."

"Some poor family is probably crying right now because their cat is missing."

"I don't think so," said Ben. "I think maybe they're glad he's gone. He's not such a nice cat. He bit me four times."

"Well, as long as he's here, why don't you give him some milk? And while you're out in the kitchen, bring me some cookies if you didn't eat them all."

Ben was very glad he had saved two.

PHOEBE SAT BEHIND HER DESK, watching the wall clock that was conveniently facing her. When the clock reached four, she knew that her children would be home and wondering what had happened to her. She wondered if she could ask to go home early. In order to get home, though, she would need a ride, and she didn't think Richie would be in the mood to offer to drive her. For the last thirty minutes, she and Richie hadn't exchanged a word.

At first, after the swearing in, everything had been fine. Tracy had gone out for some coffee for everyone and Daryl had passed around his doughnuts, and one by one, in reminiscent tones, they had traded Billy Benson stories for her entertainment. She had enjoyed herself immensely. Sitting around and having a good time with three other adults was what she was missing in her life. Staying home and cleaning her house wasn't nearly as entertaining. She was beginning to think she was going to like the job of sheriff.

But then, after about an hour, Daryl and Tracy got back to work and Richie took her into the sheriff's department office. If Phoebe had been prone to claustrophobia, that office would have given her a major case. As it was, she was sure she would find it depressing.

Picture a linoleum floor of no determinate color. Picture green walls, pockmarked here and there with flyers faded so badly they were no longer legible, the tape holding them to the wall now dried and yellow and crumbling. Picture a greasy mark on the wall behind her gray metal desk, no doubt where Billy Benson had rested his well-oiled head. Picture one window, so dirty it couldn't be seen through. Picture a fluorescent ceiling fixture that Phoebe was sure was turning her complexion the same shade of dull green as the walls.

A desk, a swivel chair, a table and a second chair against one wall, and that was it. No, not quite. There was also an overflowing wastebasket and a clock on the wall.

Phoebe, still feeling good from the conversation, not yet depressed by the office, tried a conspiratorial smile on Richie. Instead of returning it, he shrugged.

"It's due for another paint job," he said, following her gaze around the office.

"It looks as though it was due for one ten years ago," said Phoebe.

"You get used to it."

"I don't think I could," said Phoebe, trying to picture it with white walls, a rug on the floor and maybe curtains at the window. "Who's in charge of cleaning it?"

"The building has a cleaning woman. I think she mops the floor at night."

If so, thought Phoebe, she mopped it last when the mop was dirty from all the other offices. "You wouldn't mind if I fixed it up a little, would you?"

"You're the boss," said Richie.

There was a telephone on her desk that was silent. There was a CB radio on Richie's table, also silent. She sat down behind her desk and waited for something to happen. Nothing did. "What do we do now?" she asked him.

"It's a slow time of year."

"What would Sheriff Benson be doing if he were here?"

"Napping."

"That's it? Did he get a salary for that?"

"Of course," said Richie. "You get one, too."

That she would be making money hadn't occurred to her. Any salary, even a small one, would certainly make her life easier. "Are you telling me the taxpayers are paying money so that the sheriff can sit around and take naps?"

"What do you want from me, Sheriff? You want me to go out and drum up some crime to make you happy? Be happy it's slow right now. That way you'll have time to learn your job."

"And how do I do that?"

"You can start by reading the bylaws. They should be somewhere in your desk. And when you finish with those, you could read some of the old files, familiarize yourself with what we do here."

"And what're you going to be doing while I'm doing that?"

"The car's due for an oil change—I thought I'd take it in. With your permission, of course, Sheriff."

She decided that sounded like a very good idea. Being stuck in an office the size of a nine by twelve area rug all day with a man who obviously resented her didn't hold any great appeal for her. "Go ahead," she told him. "If anything comes up, I'll call you at the garage."

Richie left the office in a very big hurry.

RICHIE WAS IN A FOUL MOOD.

The new sheriff. He really didn't want to think about her, but she was someone he was going to have to get used to. Unless he quit his job, of course, or she fired him. He had a feeling, though, that she didn't know she was able to fire him. But quitting his job wouldn't be a smart move with the lack of work available in Greensboro Bend. And anyway, he liked the work. He liked dealing with people. He liked the fact that the work was always different. He even liked the quiet times of year, because they were more than made up for in the summer when the vacationers arrived.

He supposed he could always get a job in the piano factory where his cousins worked, but he knew that

Phoebe's Deputy 33

kind of monotonous work, everything the same day in, day out, would drive him crazy.

He could always move to Burlington, where there were more job opportunities, but he hated cities. People weren't friendly in cities. And in cities you couldn't own thirty-six acres of mostly pine trees that were as pretty as any picture postcard ever made of Vermont. When the day came that he retired, he could go into the Christmas tree business with no further investment at all.

He guessed he'd stick it out. What was the worst that could happen? He wasn't sure whether it would be Billy Benson somehow coming back or Phoebe Tripp staying on. It was too soon to tell. But he knew one thing for sure: at the next election, he'd be running for sheriff.

He had always thought that when Billy retired he would just move into the position of sheriff. That had been assumed, he thought, by everyone. He was sure that he could beat Phoebe in the next election. He was well liked in the area and he had the experience. And unlike Billy, he wouldn't neglect to file.

Phoebe Tripp. He didn't know quite what to make of her. One minute she was blushing and the next she was sounding like the very worst kind of housewife who probably wanted ruffled curtains on the office windows. And then in the next breath she was announcing to them over coffee and doughnuts that she wouldn't wear a gun, that she didn't believe in guns. A sheriff without a gun? That was like Vermont without snow.

Daryl had summed it up best when he had said, "Real sheriffs don't wear bras." Phoebe hadn't been around when he'd said it, of course; that had been something Daryl had said when Richie was on his way out to get the car serviced.

Richie had countered with, "Well, if that's the criterion, Daryl, we might have us a real sheriff. Her sister's part of that crazy female commune, so I wouldn't put it past her to have burned her bras with the rest of them."

Then Tracy had looked up from her typing and said, "You two are beginning to sound exactly like Billy Benson," and that had shut them up. In fact, that was about the worst thing she could say to either of them.

When it came right down to it, Richie thought, Sheriff Tripp didn't need a bra. He had no business noticing, but since he'd been stuck in a little space with an appealing female it was pretty hard not to notice. Appealing? Is that what he really thought? To be honest, yes. There was definitely something appealing about her, but it was mostly disguised by a lot of other things.

Being mad at Maggie at the moment didn't help. It was a fact that when he was mad at Maggie other women did start to appeal to him. For the third week in a row she had called him to tell him she wouldn't be home for the weekend because she was once again going skiing with her friends. Whether the friends were male or female, he didn't even inquire. He had a feeling at least some of them were male, but he'd rather not know for sure.

It wasn't easy dating a college student. So maybe she was a graduate student, but she was still twenty-four to his thirty-four, and sometimes she made him feel very old. He didn't figure the age difference would matter so much when she was thirty-four to his forty-four, but right now there was a hell of a lot of difference between someone who had been a sheriff's deputy for ten years and someone who was still in college.

Not that they had anything exclusive going. Maggie had made it clear from the beginning that she had no intention of not dating while she was at school, and she told him he was free to do as he liked. Only there wasn't very much to do in Greensboro Bend, because most of the women were married and the ones who weren't were either part of that crazy commune or else already going with someone. Or too old, like that Katie Lou who owned The Greenery and had half the men in town going gaga over her. Not that she wasn't a fine woman; it was just that Richie wanted someone he'd eventually end up marrying, and as far as he was concerned, that meant having children. If he wasn't mistaken, Katie Lou was past that age.

Maggie's saying she wasn't going to be around this weekend was exactly what he needed to top off a lousy week. Of course, it was only Wednesday, but he couldn't see the week improving.

Well, having a female sheriff ought to be interesting, anyway. It would give everyone something new to talk about for a while. And God knows, they could use something new to talk about.

But damn Maggie for going skiing again just when he needed her.

THE REAL BLOW CAME when Richie returned to the office at two o'clock. Granted, he had taken his time getting the car serviced, hanging around afterward to joke with the mechanics and answer their questions about the new sheriff. And then he had gone for a late lunch, prolonging the time when he would have to go back to the office and maybe take some orders from his new boss.

But what did he see when he did get back? Daryl putting the last coat of paint on the office door, Tracy and Phoebe laying floor tiles and an office that was no longer recognizable as a sheriff's office.

Phoebe looked up and saw him. "Hi, I hope you don't mind. If you want to help you could wash the window," she told him.

"You're going to need to scrape off the paint first," Daryl said. "I forgot to pick up some razor blades."

Richie would be damned if he was going to wash windows. That wasn't part of the work of a deputy. "You sure work fast," he said to Phoebe, meaning it in more ways than one. She had a lot of nerve just walking in and changing everything to suit herself. It kind of reminded him of women who saw his house for the first time and immediately wanted to redecorate it.

"It doesn't take long to do a room this size," said Phoebe, "and now we'll have a pleasant place in which to work."

Richie wheeled around and left the office before he said something he'd regret later. He'd buy the razor blades and even scrape the paint off the glass, but he wasn't about to wash windows. She could damn well do that herself.

By three-thirty the office was finished. The walls and ceiling were white; the floor was laid with tiles that resembled white bricks; a cheery wall calendar and two prints of floral arrangements hung on the walls; yellow curtains appeared to bring in sunlight even with the sky overcast; yellow plastic pencil holders and other desk accessories brightened up the gray desks.

Phoebe's Deputy 37

The new office depressed the hell out of Richie; he felt as if he were in a girls' dormitory.

She was going to make them the laughingstock of Vermont, that's what. Just wait until the state troopers got a load of the office, they would be laughing all the way to Montpelier. Just the sight of it would have been enough to send Billy on a month's bender.

"Isn't it darling?" asked Tracy, looking around in admiration at the new office.

"Adorable," agreed Richie.

Daryl was giving him an evil grin. "Cutest little sheriff's office I've ever seen."

"It's clean and bright and cheerful," said Phoebe, "and that's what's important."

The piano factory was sounding better to Richie by the moment.

HE HAD BEEN SITTING with his back to her for the past half-hour. Maybe he was counting the petals on the flowers in the picture over his table. Maybe, but what Phoebe called it was a sulk. For some reason it was very evident that Richie didn't like the new office decor, and since the new office decor was a great improvement over the old office decor, his sullenness had to be more personal than that. It had to be resentment over her coming in and changing it, which all added up to a sulk.

When her children sulked she was always able to humor them out of it. She couldn't do that with Richie. She couldn't treat him like Ben and go over and pick him up and give him a kiss and say, "Who does Mommy love to death?" If she did that, he'd probably have her committed. Or she couldn't, as she would with Dory, start talking to him in crossword puzzle language. She couldn't say, "What's a four-letter word for sitting with your back to me and ignoring me?" That just wouldn't work.

Apologizing might work, but she didn't feel she had anything to apologize for. Certainly painting the office had been more productive than napping. She hadn't been goofing off, if that's what he thought. She had read the bylaws. She had even looked through the files. But after that there had been nothing at all to do but stare at the four dirty walls and think about what she could do to improve them.

It was too late to worry about it now. The office was done and if Richie felt like sulking about it, fine. What she had to do was get home to her children.

She cleared her throat, and when it got no response from him, she said, "I have to get home. My children don't know about me being sheriff and they'll be worried."

That got a response from him, anyway. Swiveling around in his chair to face her, he said, "Children?" He made it sound like a word in a foreign language.

"Yes. I'll make some arrangements after today, but if you could give me a ride home, I'd appreciate it."

"That car's yours as long as you're sheriff. I can get a ride home with Daryl."

"You don't mind if I leave early?"

"You're the boss, Sheriff. You can leave anytime you want."

That didn't answer the question, but she supposed it would have to do. Tomorrow she would work on getting on better terms with her deputy. And maybe by tomorrow he'd be over the sulks.

"I'll see you in the morning, then," said Phoebe.

He had a sarcastic I-can-hardly-wait look on his face, but all he said was "Fine."

"WHAT'S A SIX-LETTER WORD meaning a banquet in honor of some person or event?" asked her mother, and Dory set aside the crossword puzzle she was working on and said, "Dinner."

Her mom was being cute again. Her mom thought that since Dory spent a lot of time doing crossword puzzles, the way to get her attention was to ask that kind of question. Her mom had never done a crossword puzzle in her life and didn't understand in the least what they were all about.

The thing about crossword puzzles was that they were perfect. They began with blanks and you filled them in, and when you were finished you had a perfect whole. If you made a mistake and put the wrong word in, though, then nothing fit right and instead of perfection you got chaos. That was one of the words she learned from doing crossword puzzles—chaos.

Crossword puzzles were a lot like families. You take an empty square, say a house, and then you fill it in with a father and a mother and two children and maybe a pet, although that wasn't absolutely necessary, and the end result was a perfect family. Whole, entire, without any missing letters or empty spaces. But remove one of those members and you ended up with chaos. Or a little brother who brought home other people's pets and a mother who spent most of her time sleeping.

Dory went out to the kitchen and saw that her mother had set candles on the table and lit them as though maybe it were someone's birthday or an anniversary. Not that there were any anniversaries anymore, and it sure wasn't any of their birthdays.

"What are we celebrating?" she asked. "You being elected sheriff?"

Her mother's cheeks and nose turned a little pink. "I know it's silly," she said, "but I thought we ought to make the best of it."

"How much money will you be making?" Dory asked her.

The pink deepened. "I didn't even ask, but compared to now, we'll be rich."

"We can have a television set again," said Ben.

Her mother shook her head. "No, Ben. The reason we don't have a television set isn't that we can't afford it."

"I thought it was," said Ben, looking betrayed.

Dory said, "It's that it's bad for our minds. People who watch TV all the time end up like vegetables." She had heard her father say that to her mother one time when they were watching television together.

"That's not true," said Ben, getting excited. "All my friends watch TV and they're not vegetables. My teacher even watches it."

A black blur flew through the air and landed on the kitchen counter next to the roast chicken that was cooling. He had his teeth embedded in the skin before her mother yelled, "Ben, get that cat off of there!"

Ben appeared to be too excited to move, so Dory went over, grabbed the cat and set him on the floor. A large piece of skin hung from his mouth and he ran out of the room and back up the stairs to the sleeping loft.

"Ben," said her mom, "you'll have to return that cat first thing in the morning."

"That cat wants to live here," said Ben.

"Maybe if you got Ben a TV set he'd quit bringing home cats," said Dory.

"No, I wouldn't," said Ben.

While her mother piled food on their plates and set them on the table, Dory poured out milk for her and Ben and coffee for her mother. When they were all seated she asked, "What happened today? Did you actually work as a sheriff?"

"Not really," said Mom. "They swore me in, but about all I did after that was fix up the office. I can't wait for you to see it. It's yellow and white and very cheerful."

"Did you get a gun?" Ben asked his mother.

"I don't approve of guns."

"You don't prove of them?"

Her mother shook her head. "No, I don't. If my deputy wants to use one that's fine, but I told him I refuse to carry one."

"I'll bet that went over big," said Dory.

"I don't think he took me very seriously anyway. I'm sure that something will be done and Sheriff Benson will be back on the job soon. I just don't know how I could be gone from nine to five every day."

"I imagine it would cut in on your sleeping time," said Dory, then was sorry she had said it when she saw her mother's stricken look. "Anyway, who would get us off in the morning?"

"While I'm sheriff, though," said her mother, "I'd like the two of you to come down to the sheriff's department after school and wait for me, and then I'll drive you home." Before Dory could protest, she added, "You can do your crossword puzzles just as well down there. And Ben will enjoy it, I think."

"I'll learn to shoot a gun," said Ben.

"Never mind guns," said their mom, "but you can learn to work the radio. That would be a big help to me. My deputy tried to explain it to me, but I couldn't get the hang of it."

Dory thought the whole business of her mother being sheriff was exceedingly laughable. She couldn't even discipline them, and she was going to have to discipline an entire county? Not that she and Ben needed much disciplining, but if they did her mother would really be in trouble. Plus she let people like Aunt Mavis boss her around all the time and she couldn't even stand up to her own mother.

Her father now—he would have made a good sheriff. He was the one who had always given all the orders around the house and made sure everyone did his own share of the work. But she didn't want to think about her father. It didn't do any good at all thinking about him, because he was never coming back and that was that.

"Dory, you're not eating," said her mother.

"I'm not hungry." Thinking about her father sometimes did that to her.

"Are you dieting?"

Her mother had put so much anxiety into that question that it made Dory mad and she started to eat. Of course she wasn't dieting. Why should she diet? She was getting nice and plump, just the way she wanted to be. She'd far rather be fat than skinny. Skinny people, like her mom, just weren't strong enough.

She knew, though, that her eating was very much like her mother's sleeping and Ben's bringing home cats. Her father's leaving had left an empty spot in all of them that they were desperately trying to fill.

PHOEBE NEEDED TO TALK to a mother. She wanted advice, reassurance, all kinds of things that a mother was supposed to provide. Only her old mother, Kathryn Louise Parker, homemaker and faculty wife in Princeton, New Jersey, was gone, and in her place was Katie Lou, tavern owner and high liver and someone who didn't seem very much like a mother at all anymore.

Her mother's tavern was only two miles up the road, but it could have been two hundred as far as Phoebe was concerned. Only once had she visited The Greenery, and that had been enough. Her once sedate mother who had played classical music on the piano had been sitting at an old upright, belting out a song to the raucous cheers of the customers. A banjo player and a fiddler, both of them hardly over twenty-one, had been accompanying her.

Phoebe had stood by the entrance, waiting for her mother to finish playing and singing, when a man in overalls and a bushy beard had asked her to dance. She hadn't even talked to a man since Ted had left her and she had panicked, fleeing the tavern and never returning.

Not that she didn't see her mother occasionally, and of course on holidays, but she only saw her when her mother chose to drop by. Since Phoebe didn't have a telephone she couldn't call her, and since her mother had taken to going out with men, Phoebe hesitated to drop in on her unexpectedly.

Ben was in bed along with the visiting cat, Dory was doing her homework at the kitchen table and Phoebe was just sitting in the living room, fretting and longing for a mother who no longer existed.

Of course, nothing was stopping her from getting into her sheriff's car and driving over to the tavern to see her mother. It was a week night, which probably meant there would be no live music and no crowds. The place might even be empty. Maybe her mother was just sitting around, wishing someone would walk in so she'd have someone to talk to. She might even be missing a daughter the way Phoebe was missing a mother.

Only she doubted it. There were probably at least ten men there, all vying for her attention.

Still, she was still the same mom who had rocked her and comforted her when she was small and Mavis had done something mean to her. She was still the same mom who had read stories to her when Mavis and her dad had been playing chess together. She might be thinner now and dress more like a sister than a housewife. She might have long straight hair with all traces of gray gone instead of short, permanented curls. She might have developed an outgoing personality now that she was out on her own. She might outwardly be almost a totally different person, but she knew that somewhere inside her old mother still resided and she'd be there for her if Phoebe needed her.

And Phoebe did need her.

She got up and walked to the kitchen. "I'm thinking of taking a drive over to see Grandma," she told Dory.

"Okay, Mom."

"You'll be all right?"

"Of course. Tell her hello for me."

"You sure you don't mind my going?"

"Mom," she said, sounding exasperated, "go on. You don't have to be here with us every minute."

"If you're positive."

Dory gave her a despairing look. "Just get out of here, will you?"

Phoebe had been hoping her daughter would beg her to stay home.

"Go on, Mom, Grandma's probably dying to congratulate you. I'll bet she'll be really proud that you're the new sheriff."

"You really think so, Dory?"

"Absolutely."

"Well, in that case," said Phoebe, but not quite believing Dory. She had a feeling that instead of being proud of her, her mother would somehow find it peculiar.

Phoebe found it pretty peculiar herself.

Chapter Three

After a wild day of celebration at the Crazy Quilt Women's Commune, which culminated in everyone standing in a circle, holding hands and singing a rousing rendition of "We Shall Overcome," the women held an action meeting.

It was a rather small meeting, since the community had dwindled to only five members. There was Mavis, who, although she swore they were all equal and didn't have leaders, was, in effect, the leader by virtue of the fact she could talk louder and longer than any of the other women. Then there were the Joandaughter twins, Peggy and Patsy, in their late thirties and the only members of the commune who knew how to run a farm; Deborah (no last name), thirty-two, a painter of women's portraits who didn't get many commissions since she always made her subjects look older than they were; and Marian Tasty, forty, the rather successful writer of health-food cookbooks, who, Mavis was sure, would be the next to move out and had already been seen perusing the real estate section of the paper.

The commune had lost three members in just the past month: one to marriage, which was a shock to the community, since they hadn't even known she was dating; one to a better job offer in Boston; and the third to a sanctuary group in Burlington.

Once the meeting was loosely called to order, Mavis took over. "The beauty of it is—" she pointed out to the others "—we now own the sheriff of Orleans County. I'd say that pretty much gives us the power around here."

"Doesn't that make us just like the men?" asked Peggy, and Patsy immediately nodded her agreement.

Mavis, never one to tolerate differences of opinion when those differences were of her opinions, frowned. "Of course it does. Isn't that the point? We want equality, don't we?"

"I think what Peggy means," said Patsy, "is that makes us as bad as they are. We have to show that we can use our power better than the men."

"We will use it better," said Mavis. "We'll use it to help women." She looked around to see if she was going to get any arguments over that, and when she saw she wasn't, she said, "First of all, it means we can go ahead with our recruitment campaign. And if those rednecks show up again and start hassling us, my sister, as sheriff of this county, will ensure that law and order are maintained. Which will be a decided improvement over Billy Benson, who arrived drunk and announced it was open season on man-haters."

"Amen to that," murmured Deborah, which drew some glances, since the commune had no religious orientation. Noticing the glances, she amended it to, "Right on!"

"I think what we should do," said Marian, "is drive over to your sister's place right now and offer our congratulations."

Mavis thought that was about the last thing they should do. She had a pretty good idea what Phoebe's feelings toward her would be at the moment. But was it her fault that idiot Billy Benson had neglected to file?

"I have a better idea," Mavis told them. "I think we should all go down to the sheriff's department tomorrow and officially welcome our new sheriff. Anyway, knowing Phoebe, she's no doubt in bed by now."

"We could take some flowers," said Patsy, whose greenhouse bloomed all year round.

Mavis, who thought flowers were a stupid idea, merely nodded at that suggestion. "I think the main thing we should do—right after congratulating her, of course—is make another formal protest about that drifter who's set up camp in the cemetery backing our property. I think the only reason Billy Benson didn't run him off—as he should have—is that they got drunk together and after that Billy no doubt regarded him as a buddy."

"We definitely have to get rid of him," said Deborah. "I've seen him watching us and it's making me nervous."

He was watching them all right, thought Mavis. Watching them and laughing at them. The nerve of the man, just walking in one day and pitching his tent on consecrated ground and right in view of their commune. She figured he had to be a drunk. She couldn't think of who else could survive a Vermont winter in a tent. All winter she had been hoping that one night he would freeze to death in his sleep, but so far they hadn't been that lucky.

Most important, though, was making up with Phoebe. Not because of any sisterly love, but because if she didn't, that niece and nephew of hers would be left to grow up without the influence of a real feminist.

Oh, Phoebe was a feminist of sorts, she'd grant her that, but Mavis had caught her backsliding on several occasions, the most recent of which had been Christmas, when the children had been given sexist gifts. The most shocking example had been the GI Joe doll that Ben had received. The fact that it was a doll did nothing to offset the warlike nature of the gift. And that book, *Seventeen Magazine's Beauty Tips for Teenagers*, for thirteen-year-old Dory? As though girls should have to worry about how they looked for boys. She knew for damned sure boys didn't get books on how to look good for girls. Although she had a suspicion that Phoebe had bought that book for herself. Phoebe had never been above sneaking on a little makeup even though when she had lived in the commune she had adhered to the natural look.

Actually, Phoebe ought to be thanking her about this time. She was going to be getting out of the house and meeting people and getting paid for it in the bargain. It was just that she knew Phoebe, and Phoebe never appreciated anything Mavis did for her. She hadn't appreciated her when they were growing up and Mavis had tried to give her advice on how to be more popular. She hadn't appreciated her when Mavis had told her not to marry Ted because he'd bore her to death. She hadn't appreciated her when Mavis had flown in to supervise her divorce—in fact, Phoebe had felt guilty about taking any money from Ted at all. And she hadn't appreciated her when they'd lived in the commune and Mavis had tried to take the children's education in hand. She guessed she shouldn't be surprised if Phoebe also didn't appreciate being elected sheriff. Phoebe never knew what was good for her.

All in all, though, even if she wasn't shown any appreciation for it, it was a day to congratulate herself. It had been her idea that Phoebe run for sheriff, and by God, she had pulled it off.

If they played their cards right, Orleans County would be theirs.

"DID YOU HEAR THE JOKE about the new sheriff?"

"Watch it, Frank," said Katie Lou. "That's my daughter you're talking about."

Frank did a double take as did the other two state troopers seated next to him. "The sheriff is your daughter?"

"That's right, boys."

"But her name's Tripp."

"That was her married name," Katie Lou informed them.

Frank looked down to the far end of the bar, where the recently deposed sheriff, Billy Benson, was tying one on. "Does Billy know?"

"I don't recall mentioning it to him," said Katie Lou with a grin. "Not that everyone isn't going to know soon enough, but I didn't see any point in making a big deal out of it."

"Hell, Katie, luv," said Frank, "a person would think you could at least buy drinks for the house, an occasion like this and all."

"I'll buy the three of you drinks," she told him, "and we'll have a quiet little toast of our own." No free drinks for Billy; Billy had had enough.

She set out four shot glasses on the bar and filled them with her best whiskey, then refilled the mugs of

Phoebe's Deputy 51

draft beer for chasers. They were all raising their shot glasses while waiting for Frank to finish his maudlin toast, when the door to The Greenery opened and in walked Phoebe herself, looking, as usual, like something the cat dragged in. Katie Lou just couldn't imagine where her daughter managed to find such ugly clothes, even in Greensboro Bend.

Frank, who had looked around to see what had caught Katie Lou's attention, yelled out, "Speak of the devil—it's the new sheriff, folks."

"I didn't know you knew who my daughter was," said Katie Lou.

"She may try to be a hermit," Frank said, "but I know every woman within a fifty-mile radius of this place. I just didn't know she was your daughter."

Katie Lou noted that Phoebe looked ready to bolt, while at the same time she saw that Billy Benson seemed to have roused himself. Moving quickly from behind the bar, she got to the door before Phoebe could run out of it. "We were just drinking a toast to you, sweetie. Come on in and have a drink on the house."

"Just coffee, Mom, if you have it."

"Nonsense. One drink isn't going to set you on the path to hell, Phoebe. In fact, I think the whole place ought to drink a toast to you. Of course, I can't guarantee Billy Benson will drink to your success."

Phoebe, naturally, was turning varying shades of red as she always did. She took after her father in that respect. But, then, Phoebe took after her father in a lot of respects. "The sheriff's here?" she asked, panic showing in her eyes.

"You're the sheriff, honey, but if you mean Billy Benson, that's him at the end of the bar. The one who'd be falling off the barstool if his feet weren't wrapped around the rungs."

She dragged Phoebe over to the bar, ordered her to sit down and poured her a beer. A whiskey on the side might be going a little far.

"Hey, boys," she yelled to a couple of the locals sitting at one of the tables. "Come on over and meet the new sheriff. And don't be shy, she's my daughter."

"Mother, please," Phoebe murmured, but Katie Lou ignored her.

"Be a good sport, Billy, and come on down here to this end of the bar and meet my daughter, the new sheriff," yelled Katie Lou, thinking it was better they met sooner rather than later.

Fortunately Billy seemed too drunk to care who he was meeting. He fumbled his way down the bar, his unabashed pot belly hanging out and covering his belt, his small feet, encased in his boots, seeming too small to carry all the weight. His droopy eyelids were at half-mast and he needed a shave. He stopped in front of the stool on which Phoebe was sitting, squinted up at her with bloodshot eyes and said, "You sure don't look like your mother."

"She takes after her father," said Katie Lou, adding, as an afterthought, "A fine-looking man, he was."

Billy wasn't finished. "You sure don't look like a sheriff, either."

"At least she's in shape, Billy Benson, and not falling down drunk," Katie Lou told him.

"I had no intention of winning," Phoebe said to Billy.

"Don't apologize to him," said Katie Lou. "You not only won, you're the better man." Then, seeing Phoebe's blush, she amended it to, "The better sheriff, anyway."

"Mother, do you think we could talk for a few minutes? In private?"

"Frank, take over for a few minutes, will you?" Katie Lou said. Then she led Phoebe to the back, where she had a small office. She waited while Phoebe sat down, then went around and sat behind the desk. "What is it, honey?" Her daughter looked as nervous as a cheating husband whose wife had just walked into the tavern and caught him with his girlfriend.

Phoebe reached into her pocket, took out a pack of cigarettes and pulled one out, then spent moments hunting in her pockets for something to light it with. Katie Lou finally got impatient, found some matches in her desk drawer and lit it for Phoebe. She even abstained from her usual lecture about smoking.

"I don't know what to do, Mom. Mavis talked me into this, but she swore I wouldn't actually be elected. Now I don't know how to get out of it."

"Out of it? Why should you want to get out of it? I think you'll make a great sheriff, Phoebe."

"Me? I can't even shoot a gun."

"That's what you have a deputy for. You met the old sheriff out there. That was one of his more lucid moments. Do you honestly think you can't do better than that?"

"My deputy already resents working for me. It's not as though a lot of people voted for me. It was an accident I got elected and he knows it."

"You talking about Richie Stuart?"

Phoebe nodded.

"He seems like a good man, Phoebe. I don't see why he'd give you any trouble."

"I heard," began Phoebe, then looked away and closed her mouth.

"You heard what?"

"Forget it, Mom, it's none of my business."

"What'd you hear, Phoebe? Tell your mother."

"I heard you were dating some law enforcement person. I was wondering if it was Richie."

Katie Lou could barely contain her smile. The way her daughter was blushing she would swear she had some personal interest in her deputy and had gotten the idea he was her mother's boyfriend.

"Afraid not, Phoebe. It's Frank out there I've been seeing. He's a state trooper, not a sheriff's deputy. And it's nothing serious, not even worth talking about. And if it ever was serious, honey, I wouldn't keep it a secret from you."

Phoebe seemed to cheer up at that news, but then her mouth turned back down. "I don't see how I can be sheriff, Mom. I have to be home with the kids."

"Nonsense. Your kids will be fine. There are a lot of working mothers out there, Phoebe."

"You didn't work."

Katie Lou sighed. "No, I didn't, but times have changed. Your father expected me to stay home and I did, but now that I see what fun it can be to run my own business, I wish I had done it years ago."

"You don't mean that."

"I certainly do, Phoebe. Anyway, your children are in school all day. And come summer you'll have enough money to send them to camp. Or get a housekeeper."

Phoebe didn't look convinced. "It should be Mavis, not me. Mavis is much better at giving orders."

"That's true enough, but there's more to being sheriff than giving orders. And personally, I'd rather take orders from you than from Mavis. I don't know how I got such a bossy daughter—or one as unassuming as you, for that matter. Maybe *I* should have run for sheriff."

Phoebe smiled, and in that moment she reminded Katie Lou so much of her late husband she had to blink. Prettier, of course, but that same sweet smile that practically caused a meltdown in her heart. "You ought to stop by more often, honey. I miss seeing you."

"I would, Mom, but I don't feel at ease in bars."

"Neither do I, which is why I bought my own. But with me here, I would think you'd be able to consider this your second home. Anyway, your constituents hang out here and you ought to get to know them. In fact, they'll think you're undemocratic if you stay away. I tell you what, Phoebe. Saturday night I'll have a little celebration here in your honor, introduce you to all the people you'll need to meet. I'll even invite your sister, but I hope she'll leave that group of hers at home."

"The group's fine when they're not around Mavis, Mom. She's the rabble-rouser of the bunch."

"She always was, wasn't she?" And where Mavis got that from, she'd never know.

"Never mind a party, Mom. It's not necessary. Anyway, I don't like leaving the kids alone."

"No excuses, Phoebe—bring them along. I don't see enough of them, either. Anyway, you used to baby-sit at Dory's age. You've got to stop smothering them.''

"I don't smother them."

"Well, you've got to start living your own life. In a few years, at the rate you're going, people around here will be calling you the hermit lady."

"I like staying home with the kids."

"Of course you do. But you could find some time to spend with your poor old mother, too."

That got a chuckle out of Phoebe. "You? A poor old mother?"

"Don't go by exteriors, Phoebe. Beneath this gorgeous, incredibly youthful facade lurks a grandmother, you know."

That got a real belly laugh from Phoebe.

"And I didn't bring it up before because I thought maybe it was too soon, but it wouldn't hurt to get out and meet some men, Phoebe."

"I'm not interested."

"Well, granted, there's not much around here to be interested in, but you're not the type of woman to be happy living alone the rest of your life. Mavis I can see being without a man, and the men are probably better off because of it. But not you, honey." She would have suggested Richie to her, especially since Phoebe had already mentioned him, but she remembered seeing Richie in The Greenery with a cute young blonde. And a cute young blonde would no doubt appeal to Richie more than a woman with two children. Men were like that; they never knew a good thing when they saw it.

After Phoebe left, Katie Lou threw everyone out and closed up early. She was worried about Phoebe. She always worried about Phoebe. She would have thought it would be Mavis with her crazy ways she'd worry about, but Mavis could take care of herself.

Phoebe had always been the shy one. The one who had made above-average grades in school, but only by pushing herself, and then was made to feel she was slow because Mavis achieved all A's with no effort at all. And Phoebe had always been on the outside of the social life looking in, while Mavis, in those days before she became a feminist, was always besieged by boys begging her to go out with them.

She and Phoebe's father had been so happy when Phoebe had fallen in love with one of her father's teaching assistants and gotten married. That was all Phoebe had ever really wanted: to get married and have her own family. But Katie Lou had seen the trouble in the marriage long before anyone else had.

Maybe it was Ted who ultimately broke up the marriage, but it had been Phoebe who had precipitated it. She had tried so hard to be a good wife, was so zealous in her attempts to please Ted, to be everything he wanted, that Katie Lou was sure he must have finally felt smothered by all the love and attention, just as Phoebe's children would no doubt feel the same way if they remained her entire world, as they had been since Ted had left her.

Phoebe had never held an opinion of her own in her married days. It was always "Ted thinks this" or "Ted wants us to do that," until Katie Lou had to wonder after a while whether her younger daughter even had a mind of her own.

Mavis's getting Phoebe to run for sheriff was probably the only good thing she had ever done for her sister. Katie Lou hoped Phoebe would stick it out. It was the kind of thing that might give her enough independence that she'd be able to hold her own with a man. She also thought she might make a damn fine sheriff.

But, then, after Billy Benson, anyone would have to look good.

RICHIE WAS SURPRISED to find Maggie in. Most of the time when he tried to call her at the university she would be out, and later she'd say she'd been to the library, studying. Richie had a feeling she didn't do all that much studying, but didn't think he had a right to question her.

"What's happening, Richie?" she asked right off.

"Just felt like hearing your voice, Maggie."

"You just called to hear my voice?"

"Isn't that allowed?"

"You're lucky you caught me in. I have an exam tomorrow and I'm home studying."

"What's new?" asked Richie, not really wanting to know but hoping she'd ask him the same.

"Six more inches of good snow, that's what. I know I've said it before, but it seems such a waste for you to live in Vermont and not ski."

Not wanting to get into that discussion again, he just blurted it out. "We've got a new sheriff."

"You're kidding. You mean Billy's out? What happened?"

"We had an election, that's what happened. And stupid Billy forgot to file. So by default we got us this female sheriff."

"Hey, that's terrific. You mean a woman actually won? In Orleans County?"

"I told you, Maggie, it was by default."

"Well, good for her. Anyone I know?"

Phoebe's Deputy

"Her name's Phoebe Tripp."

"I don't think I know her. Hey, you ought to be out celebrating. You've finally seen the last of Billy."

"Well, I'm not sure this new one's any improvement."

"Come on, Richie, how could she not be an improvement?"

"There's something about taking orders from a woman," he said, being honest, then realizing too late that being that honest with Maggie might not be such a good idea.

It wasn't. "Did I hear you correctly, Richie?"

"Well, it's just—hell, Maggie, I've never worked for a woman before."

"Do you find her inferior in some way because she's a woman?"

"I didn't say that, Maggie."

"No, but I'm reading between the lines. What you're really saying is an inept drunk like Billy is preferable to any woman."

"Just listen to me for a moment. Let me give you an example. You know what the first thing she did was?"

"Don't tell me she fired you."

"No. But that might be the second thing. The first thing was, she redecorated the office."

"Good for her. That place was a dump, Richie. I felt like I was going to catch something every time I stopped by to see you."

"Okay, so it was dirty. I'll admit that. But get this, we've now got yellow curtains at the window. In a sheriff's office!"

"What's really bothering you, Richie?"

"I just told you."

"No. Yellow curtains aren't the issue. If Billy had put in yellow curtains you wouldn't have blinked an eye."

"Billy wouldn't have put in yellow curtains."

"I can't believe this sudden loyalty to Billy. You've been hoping he'd disappear from the scene ever since I met you. Or is that it? Were you hoping to be the next sheriff?"

"Well, of course I was, and don't make it sound so unnatural."

"Then why didn't you run?"

"You know damn well why I didn't run. Because if I'd lost, Billy would've fired me. Anyway, I figured he'd retire in another couple of years."

"Okay, Richie, if that's the real reason, if it's not just that you resent working for a woman, then why don't you try getting a job with the state police? Or another sheriff's department?"

"Don't think I'm not considering it. But I can't just quit on her now. She doesn't know the first thing about the job, I'd be leaving the county with no protection at all."

"Those are really noble sentiments, Richie. Pardon me if I don't quite believe them."

"Well, you're wrong if you don't believe me, because that's the truth. I've been a deputy here for ten years. I'm not going to just walk out now before Phoebe even knows what she's doing."

"Is she good-looking?"

"What the hell has that got to do with it?"

"Just asked a question, that's all."

"She's tall and skinny and has red hair that's so bushy it looks like a man's beard. Plus she has children."

"Does she also have a husband?"

"I don't know. She didn't mention one. But, then, we really didn't get personal."

"How old is she?"

"About my age. What is this, you jealous?" He was hoping she'd say yes, but knew she'd say no.

"Don't be stupid, Richie. And don't be stupid about her, either. Give her a chance, why don't you? At least it'll be a change for you."

"Why don't you change your mind and come home this weekend?"

"It's tempting. I'd like to meet the new sheriff. But our plans are made and it's too late to cancel them. Next weekend, though, I'll be down for sure. You going to introduce me to the new sheriff?"

"If I'm still working for her by then, sure."

"Hang in there, Richie, maybe she'll teach you a thing or two."

Teach him something? That crazy new sheriff? That'd be the day. Anyone who put up yellow curtains in the sheriff's department had nothing to teach him at all.

He wondered if seeing Maggie wasn't a dead end, though. Once she got her master's degree in psychology she would be looking for a job, and psychologists weren't in demand in Greensboro Bend. The only thing that might keep her there was the skiing, but Richie didn't think that would be enough.

He also had a feeling he'd been kidding himself that she'd marry him and settle down.

Next time she came down he'd get her to talk about it. Up until now he hadn't pushed it because he didn't want to lose her, but maybe he ought to find out where he stood, because it might be he was going to lose her anyway.

And where would that leave him? Back to trying to find an eligible woman in a town so small that sometimes the only eligible woman turned out to be your sister.

He had this dream, but maybe that was all it would ever be. When he had first bought his property all it had had on it was a small log cabin. He had spent his weekends that first year enlarging the cabin to give him a little more space. It had turned out that he enjoyed the actual work more than he needed the space. After that he had added another bedroom, which he used as a den, and then a second bathroom so that guests wouldn't see how messy his own bathroom was.

By that time he was hooked on building things. He built a garage for his car and a storage shed for his tools, and his third summer in the house he had added a screened porch to the back so that he could sit out in the evenings and admire his property without being bitten to death.

He would sit out there and picture himself married with a bunch of kids. As each one outgrew his crib, he would add on another bedroom, maybe a playroom. And there would be tree houses to build and maybe a playhouse for the girls, and down by his stream he could put in a gazebo.

And at Christmas he would take his kids into the woods and have them pick out which tree they wanted cut down, and every spring they would plant new trees. And when his wife would say, "We're running out of closet space," he could add on a couple of those.

Sometimes he could picture Maggie as his wife and sometimes he couldn't. She was fun to be with and they always had a good time when they were together, but he'd hate to marry someone who would wake up one day and realize that all she did with all her degrees was clean a house and take care of children, when she could have become a successful psychologist with enough money to pay someone else to do those things for her. And then she'd resent him, wouldn't she?

Well, maybe being a small-town sheriff and having a Christmas tree business on the side was the kind of dream that just wasn't practical. Maybe, if he really wanted a wife and family, he was going to have to get a job in a city somewhere where there'd be a variety of single women to meet.

And if he didn't, maybe he'd end up like old Billy Benson, drunk every night because he had no one to go home to.

It wasn't a pretty picture to contemplate.

Chapter Four

"Aren't you supposed to be at work, Mom?"

Phoebe looked at her daughter with an apologetic grimace. "I overslept."

"You better hustle," said Dory in a good imitation of her father.

"You could always stay home sick," said Ben.

Phoebe would love to stay home sick. She even felt sick at the idea of having to go to the sheriff's department again, only this time be expected to take over. Decorating was one thing; today something official might happen, and then what would she do?

Feeling like a sleepwalker, she made her way over to the stove and put some water on to boil. She was bound to feel better after a cup of coffee. Or maybe several cups of coffee.

"Would you drive me to school in the sheriff car?" Ben asked.

"Would you like that?"

His smile was glorious. "I'd love it. And you could put the siren on and all my friends would see us. Maybe that way I could get to play one of the good guys sometimes."

The most popular game among the eight-year-old boys was Miami Vice. It consisted of the good guys and the bad guys, the bad guys being shot by the good guys and dying in agony. Ben died well and for this reason was killed quite often.

"I don't know about the siren," said Phoebe, not remembering being told about a siren on the car.

"Just for a few seconds," begged Ben.

"I'd just as soon take the school bus, if you don't mind," Dory interrupted. Which must mean that being the sheriff's daughter didn't have the same cachet with the thirteen-year-olds. No doubt because some of those thirteen-year-olds had already had run-ins with the law.

Phoebe made her coffee, lit a cigarette and leaned against the counter. It wouldn't do to sit down. If she sat down, she might never get back up.

"You better hurry up, or I'll be late and no one will see me in the sheriff car," Ben said, but he sounded sweet about it. He hadn't yet caught on to the bossy tone his sister had perfected.

With a nod in his direction, Phoebe picked up her mug and made her way to the bathroom. She put on her pink-tinted glasses, looked in the mirror and took them off again. Her hair never failed to resemble a broom with broken bristles in the morning. The only time her hair looked presentable was right after she washed it, but it was too cold to go out with a wet head and her hair dryer had given up the good fight a long time ago. It usually didn't matter, since the few times she went out, she wore her knit hat over her hair. Perhaps the sheriff wore a hat. In Westerns he always did. If she could insist on a hat then she wouldn't have to worry about her hair every morning.

She washed her face and put on mascara by feel. Then she put on her glasses to see if she had smeared it. After that came the pink lipstick that Katie Lou had given Dory for Christmas and that Dory had disdained.

Except for wearing a different color turtleneck, she dressed exactly as she had dressed the day before. However, this time she didn't wear her bedroom slippers. She should have asked if she got a uniform. Richie had been wearing khaki pants and shirt, but maybe they were just his regular clothes. She thought she might like a uniform to go with her hat. With a uniform on, people would be more likely to take her seriously as a sheriff.

She couldn't find her sheriff's badge anywhere. Back in the kitchen she saw that it was pinned on Ben's shirt. "I'll need the badge," she told him.

"Couldn't I just wear it today?"

"No. You can wear it on Saturday. And get that cat, because he's going back to wherever you found him."

Ben looked doubly crushed at two orders from her at one time. Dory looked amused, as though she were sure her mother wouldn't be capable of carrying through on either one.

"On the double," Phoebe ordered Ben, attempting to sound like a person of authority.

"Excellent," murmured Dory, then gave her mother a hug before heading out the door.

Phoebe went out to warm up the car, and minutes later Ben appeared with a moving bulge beneath his jacket. Phoebe was ready to tell him to put on his seat belt, but, afraid that it might strangle the cat, she didn't.

"Show me where you found the cat," she said.

Phoebe's Deputy 67

"It's on the way to the school bus. I'll show you."

She drove slowly up the road, loving the fact that the car was automatic and she didn't have to shift all the time. Not having to shift would make it much easier to smoke while she drove around on her duties. Maybe she'd try some of those skinny little cigars. Being dressed in a uniform and a hat and smoking a skinny cigar would make her look like a real sheriff. She wouldn't have to inhale the cigars, of course.

"There's where I found him," Ben finally said.

Phoebe pulled up in front of the farmhouse set back from the road. "Apologize for stealing their cat," she coached him.

"I didn't steal him," Ben said, getting out of the car and trotting in the direction of the house.

Phoebe watched as a door opened, and then Ben was hurrying back to the car. When he got in, he said, "They didn't even miss him. The lady said they have so many cats she can't keep track of them."

"It's a farm cat, Ben. It wouldn't be happy living in our house."

"He was so happy. He liked sleeping in my bed. And if we ever got any mice he'd catch them. Or rats. Big rats. If we got some of those he'd chase them away."

To get his mind off the cat, Phoebe said, "Why don't you see if you can figure out how to turn the siren on, honey?"

Ben's tirade about the cat subsided as he started in on a new subject, at the same time searching the dashboard for something to turn on.

"What makes a siren work, Mom?"

"What they do, Ben, is make a recording of a siren on a cassette. Then, when you push the button, the cassette starts playing and it sounds just like a siren."

"Is that really how they do it?"

"Maybe."

"Oh, okay." He was still looking for the siren when they approached his school, and just when she was about to console him for not finding it, he found it, and the resulting noise almost made her veer off the road.

She could see all the children in the schoolyard looking in their direction, and when she glanced at Ben he was sitting up in his seat looking proud as could be. When she stopped the car, he leaned over, gave her a quick kiss on the cheek, then was out of the car and strutting toward the other children. She was sure the siren had made his day.

She started up again, her right hand going to the dashboard to turn it off. Only it didn't go off. It was still blaring loudly, and all the cars ahead of her were pulling off the road and all the cars behind her were slowing down to the legal speed limit.

She tried to slouch in her seat so they couldn't see who it was with the siren on, but when she did she couldn't see out of the windshield to drive, so she had to straighten up again.

As she approached town, people came out of the buildings to see what was happening. On the one hand she felt really stupid and on the other she had enjoyed how everyone got out of her way. She even ran a stop sign, knowing that kind of behavior was allowed when a siren was being used. There hadn't been anybody coming the other way anyway.

When she got to the electric company building, though, all she felt was just plain stupid. Not only was she late for work, but she was announcing that tardiness for all to hear.

She parked by the curb and was just going to leave the car there with the siren going and hope no one noticed it, but she didn't get away with it, because no sooner had she turned off the engine than she saw Richie coming out of the door, headed in her direction.

She got out of the car and slammed the door. "Good morning," she said to him, but wasn't sure he heard her over the blare of the siren.

He nodded, opened the door and reached inside the car. The siren fizzled out.

"I didn't know how to turn it off," she explained, wondering why she felt she had to explain herself to her deputy. At least she hadn't blushed.

"How did you turn it on?" he wanted to know.

"I didn't. My son did. He wanted his friends at school to hear it."

Phoebe expected to be given a hard time about it, but all he said was "Well, you're the sheriff." He rather pointedly looked at his watch, though, and that did make her blush. But she was not about to start apologizing to him for being late, because it seemed to her she was always apologizing to someone for something and she was getting really tired of it.

She followed him inside. She exchanged good mornings with Daryl and accepted Tracy's offer to send out for coffee. Then she went into her newly painted office and sat down at her desk. She wondered what in the world she could do now that the office was all fixed up. The phone wasn't ringing;

nothing was happening. She could just as well have stayed at home in bed.

They sat in silence until Tracy arrived with the coffee, then Phoebe said to Richie, "By the way, do I get a uniform?"

"That's up to you," said Richie, "but we have to buy our own."

"Where do I get it?"

"I ordered mine out of a catalog. It's in your bottom right-hand drawer, I believe."

Phoebe found the catalog beneath several issues of the *Enquirer*. She had, of course, noticed the newspaper in grocery stores for years, but had never been able to summon up her courage to buy one. It was the kind of thing that was sure to make her blush when the checkout woman saw it. She had been known, on occasion, to blush when buying toilet paper.

Perhaps she would be able to smuggle Billy Benson's copies home and read them at her leisure.

The cover of the catalog looked very businesslike, but once she opened it up it didn't look businesslike at all. She had read somewhere that a lot of women were attracted to men in uniform. The catalog reminded her of something put out to titillate just such women.

She had personally never been drawn to men in uniform. She had never thought servicemen were cute; she had never thought of policemen as her friends; bus drivers had never held any appeal for her.

The male models—or maybe they were really officers of the law—did nothing for her. The different items being worn and displayed, however, evoked a curious reaction. She found that she was excited about the idea of wearing a uniform.

Phoebe's Deputy 71

Her eyes slid over things like helmets and holsters and rain ponchos, but returned again and again to hats and boots and low-slung belts. And after a while, she even began to view the holsters with friendliness. It wasn't as though she had to have a gun residing in one. She could even use a fake gun, just something to round out the contours of the holster.

Although she had never had a very clear image of herself, even when looking in a mirror, she now could picture herself quite easily in slim pants and boots, the gun belt low over her hips. Her khaki shirt would be open at the neck, with maybe the long sleeves rolled up, and atop her head would be a wide-brimmed hat. On her shirt pocket would reside her sheriff's badge.

She couldn't understand the sudden enthusiasm she was feeling over the possibility of wearing a uniform, and a man's uniform at that. The catalog dealt exclusively with men's clothes. She had never gone through a tomboy phase in her childhood, and her sister's current mode of dress, which was mostly combat fatigues, had never appealed to her.

She guessed it wasn't the actual clothes so much, because she already wore comfortable pants and shirts most of the time. It was what they represented. Outfitted in gear like that, people would respect her. She would represent authority.

For the first time in her life maybe someone would listen to her.

With one of the new pens and yellow legal pads she had bought the day before, she began to make a list of what she would like to order. That's when she hit a snag. She hadn't the slightest idea what size she would be in men's clothes.

She looked over at Richie. His back to her, he was leaning back in the chair tapping his fingers on the table. "Would you do me a favor, Richie?"

He took a little too long to say "Of course, Sheriff."

She had a feeling that no matter what, he was going to continue calling her "sheriff" for the rest of her life. "Would you mind standing up for a minute?"

He got slowly to his feet, looking a little uneasy as her eyes swept up and down his body. He had broad shoulders and a deep chest, which meant his shirt size would be too large for her. But she had a feeling his pants would fit her perfectly, except in length. She could be wrong, of course, but his hips looked about the same size as hers.

"What was the favor, Sheriff?"

"I'm having a problem," she told him. "I know what I want to order out of the catalog, but I don't know what my size would be in men's clothes."

"I wouldn't know that myself, Sheriff."

She looked down at his hips again, then back up at his face. "I think we might be the same size."

A twitching appeared at the corners of his mouth. "I suppose that's a possibility," he allowed.

"Do you think it would be possible... No, forget I mentioned it." She could feel her face growing warm.

Richie was beginning to smile now. She noticed that when he smiled he looked less like an Indian. Perhaps because in all the movies she had seen with Indians in them, the Indians were never smiling. "Go on, Sheriff, say what you have on your mind."

She avoided his eyes and gazed at the floral print hung above his table. "I just thought that maybe—if you didn't mind, of course—that maybe you'd let me try on your uniform to see if it fit me."

He tempered his smile, but his eyes had a spark to them. "Certainly, Sheriff. Would you like me to shut the door?"

Phoebe could feel her blush blossom forth. "No, I didn't mean . . . isn't there a men's room?"

"Down the hall and to the left."

"Perhaps you could remove your shirt and pants in there and hand them out to me. Then, after I try them on, I'll pass them back to you. Or Daryl could, if you'd prefer that." And the thought came to her that if she had a male boss and he requested that she remove her clothes so that he could try them on, she'd probably be claiming sexual harassment. And just maybe Richie would be thinking something along those lines.

But Richie appeared to be taking it as a joke, saying, "I'll trust you not to peek." And yet something about the way he said it left her wondering if he wanted to trust her not to peek. That wasn't the kind of thing she should be thinking about her deputy, whom she barely knew, so she just nodded in agreement.

She followed him down the hall to the bathroom and stood outside. Moments later he was handing out his pants and shirt through a small opening in the door. When he said, "Anything else you'd like to try on?" she ignored him, but she couldn't ignore the kind of attention she was attracting from Daryl and Tracy when she headed back to her office with Richie's clothes over her arms.

"I'm trying to figure out what size I wear," she explained.

"And probably making Richie's day," she heard Daryl murmur as she walked quickly past them to her office. She closed the door, hoping that no one would open it without first knocking.

Richie's clothes felt warm in her arms. Or perhaps her arms felt warm and were blushing along with her face, which she could tell was doing its usual thing when embarrassed. She set the clothing on the desk and sat down in her chair to remove her boots. Then she took off her jeans and tried his pants on.

In some weird way, she felt like she was doing something illegal trying on his clothes. There was a curious thrill about it, perhaps the kind of feeling transvestites got, which made them keep on doing it over and over. His pants were made of almost exactly the same kind of fabric as her jeans, and yet the fabric felt totally different against her bare legs.

Was trying on Richie's clothes going to become some secret passion of hers? Was she going crazy?

Aside from the feel, though, which had nothing to do with why she had tried them on, the fit was good. Once she rolled them up twice, the length was right, and although the waist was a little large, if she tucked in the shirt and put on a belt they would be a reasonable fit.

She tried on his shirt over her turtleneck and this time didn't feel the same sensations she had experienced when putting on his pants. The shirt was huge, but, then, she always liked her clothes roomy. And with the sleeves rolled up and two of the buttons undone, she didn't think she looked too bad.

That was pure guesswork, of course, since she didn't have a mirror, but, then, she seldom looked in mirrors while dressing. She had an image of how she looked in her mind, and when she actually saw herself in a mirror the reality never fit the image and this never failed to disconcert her.

She opened the door to the office and stepped outside to show Daryl and Tracy. "What do you think?" she asked them. She stood up straight, stuck out her chest and hooked her thumbs in her back pockets.

"You look good," said Tracy. "But you know something, Phoebe, you could go over to Willy's Store and try them on there."

"I thought I had to order them from a catalog."

Daryl shook his head. "They're just regular khakis—Willy's carries them upstairs where the men's clothes are. They have all kinds of hats, too," he added, looking at the watch cap Phoebe hadn't yet removed from her head.

"Don't they have to be official?"

"If you wear them," said Tracy, "that makes them official."

Phoebe decided that instead of going out for lunch, she'd use that time to go to Willy's and outfit herself. She was standing there, feeling pretty good about things, when she heard a banging from down the hall and then a voice shouting, "I'm freezing my butt off in here!"

Blushing scarlet, she retreated to her office.

RICHIE FELT LIKE A FOOL.

A grown man, standing in a cold public bathroom in just his underwear and socks, while that fool female sheriff was out there prancing around in his clothes. Although, to be perfectly honest—no, he didn't feel like being perfectly honest. Oh, what the hell, admit it—there was something sexy about knowing she was putting his clothes over her bare skin. Unfortunately he was in the john, with no way of seeing this sexy little episode for himself.

He'd heard all the dope on Phoebe Tripp that morning. A couple of the troopers had passed on the information to Daryl, who had passed it on to him. The news that the new sheriff was Katie Lou's daughter had been the real shocker. How a petite dark-haired woman had produced such a tall redhead for a daughter was a real mystery. Of more interest to Richie, however, was the news that the sheriff was divorced.

Not that he was personally interested in her marital status—that was about the last thing in the whole entire world that would interest him. No, it was nothing personal; it was just that he thought her being divorced would make for a better working relationship. Obviously, if she had a husband, the husband would wonder about his wife working alone all day in close quarters with a single man. It might even cause some difficulty in the marriage, or, if the husband were a certain kind of man, the uncommonly jealous kind, it could even result in a fight. Not with his wife, but with Richie. Things like that were known to happen, particularly in small towns, where everyone knew everyone else's business and the only thing to do to pass the time was to spread rumors.

For instance, he'd hate for some rumor to reach some husband that the husband's wife was trying on her deputy's clothes. The husband would probably assume that this was something Richie was enjoying. Of course it could be something he would be enjoying if he weren't in the cold bathroom and she weren't all alone in the office.

Phoebe's Deputy 77

If it had turned out, though, that she had a husband, the man wouldn't have had to worry about Richie. When it came to women, Richie was a real gentleman. And when it came to married women, Richie was more than a gentleman, he avoided them like poison ivy. He had a brother who had once gotten involved with a married woman, and it had resulted in one of the biggest messes of all time. Richie would never knowingly walk into something like that. Even if he felt like it.

Anyway, married or divorced, it meant nothing personal to Richie. He had Maggie. And maybe it was an open relationship, at least on Maggie's part. He was satisfied with it, wasn't he? He wasn't looking elsewhere, was he? Particularly at a prickly redheaded sheriff who, he was sure, meant nothing but trouble. Even if he did find her sexy for some unaccountable reason.

And all this thinking was nothing if not counterproductive, because at the moment, divorced or not, the crazy woman was parading around in his clothes while he was in real danger of catching pneumonia.

He opened his mouth to let out a yell.

LED BY MAVIS, the contingent from the Crazy Quilt Women's Commune entered the electric company building at three o'clock that afternoon. Patsy was carrying an enormous bunch of yellow jonquils. Marian was carrying a cake made with all natural ingredients. Mavis was afraid they looked more like the local women's club than a group of serious, politically minded women. Except, of course, that the members of the women's club would not be caught dead wearing combat fatigues.

Mavis noted the young woman at the desk typing. She thought it typical. A man was eyeing them from over a lowered newspaper. He had the look of a man who was trying to figure out which gender he should address them as.

"We're here to see the sheriff," said Mavis, her words for the woman at the typewriter. She always preferred dealing with a woman rather than a man when she had the option.

"Certainly," said the woman, who promptly picked up a phone and pushed a button. Mavis could then hear the sound of a telephone ringing from behind a closed door.

"Someone to see you, Phoebe," said the woman, then went back to her typing.

Moments later the closed door opened and there was Phoebe, looking much smarter than usual in khaki pants and shirt and some kind of hat that resembled something one would wear on a safari when hunting elephants. It suited her, though. She looked much more self-assured than Mavis could ever remember her looking.

Phoebe's smile was diffident, if not her attire. "Come on in my office," she invited them.

The entire commune filled the small space. Mavis took note of the man who resembled a cigar-store Indian, leaning against one wall. She had seen him around town, usually with Billy Benson, and presumed he was Billy's deputy. Phoebe's now, of course. She waited for Phoebe to speak, and when the expected chewing out wasn't forthcoming, she said, "We thought we'd come and welcome you, give you our support."

Phoebe's Deputy

Phoebe appeared to be waiting for more. Mavis looked at the others for help, but none was offered. "You look good, Phoebe," she improvised. "Much better than Billy Benson ever looked in uniform." No reason to point out that uniform pants weren't generally rolled up.

Phoebe ignored her and turned to Patsy. "What lovely flowers, Patsy, and they match the office."

That prompted Marian to set the cake down on Phoebe's desk. "I made this especially for you."

"How thoughtful," said Phoebe, still ignoring Mavis.

"All right, I take full responsibility," Mavis blurted out. "But you can't accuse me of knowing that Billy would forget to file."

"We didn't vote for you," Marian assured her.

Patsy and Peggy exchanged stricken looks. Obviously they hadn't understood they weren't to vote for Phoebe. Not that their two votes would have won it for her if Billy had filed.

Phoebe was still ignoring her.

"Okay," said Mavis, "so I got you into this. What can I say? I'm sorry, all right?"

Phoebe was being uncommonly quiet.

"Okay, I owe you one," Mavis said.

Phoebe smiled.

"And now that we have that out of the way," said Mavis, "we came here on some sheriff's business. We want to hold a rally on Saturday and we need your protection."

"Protection from what?" asked Phoebe.

"From anything. Mostly from a bunch of drunk men who have nothing better to do on Saturdays than sit around town and harass women."

"Not all the women," Marian explained. "Just us."

"What are you rallying for?" Phoebe asked.

"It's more of a membership drive," said Mavis. "We'll give a couple of speeches about communal life, maybe sing a song, and then we'll try to get some of the local women to come out and visit our farm. We need to replace some of the members we've recently lost."

"We don't work on the weekends," Phoebe said. "The state police are in charge then."

"But we need you," Mavis urged, trying to keep the commanding tone out of her voice.

"I'll tell you what. I'll come to town wearing my badge and make sure your rights to a peaceful assembly aren't violated," Phoebe said, mouthing words Mavis hadn't even known Phoebe understood.

"I'll be there, too," said the deputy, looking as though it were the kind of thing he wouldn't miss for the world.

Mavis ignored him, turning to Patsy, who was whispering, "There's that other thing."

"Yes," said Mavis, "there's one other matter. There's a drifter camping out in the local cemetery."

Phoebe looked amused. "Why would anyone camp out in a cemetery?"

"Exactly," said Mavis. "No one in his right mind would. What's worse, his tent is pitched right over the border where our land adjoins that of the cemetery. He spies on us."

"Spies on you?" asked Phoebe. "What are you doing that someone would be spying on you?"

"Maybe spying isn't the right word," said Mavis, "but he's definitely watching us. Not only do we consider it an invasion of our privacy, but I'm sure that what he's doing isn't legal. We complained to Billy about it, but all he did was go out there and get drunk with the man."

"I'll look into it," said Phoebe. "Is there anything else?"

Mavis shrugged, then shook her head. Her sister was being so damn businesslike she barely recognized her. "You doing all right, Phoebe?"

"I'm doing fine, Mavis."

Maybe it was the uniform, maybe it was the office, but whatever it was, Phoebe was acting differently. Mavis didn't think it was possible for her sister to radically change in just one day, so it had to be something else. Maybe tightly controlled fury. At her. In which case, perhaps she should make the visit brief. By the next time they met Phoebe might be enjoying her job as sheriff. Stranger things had happened, hadn't they?

Not that she could think of any at the moment.

She said, "Well, I guess we'll be going, then, Phoebe."

"Call me 'Sheriff.'"

Mavis began to grin, then saw that Phoebe was serious.

"When I'm in uniform, on the job, please address me as 'Sheriff.'"

"No need to overdo it," said Mavis. "Everyone called Sheriff Benson 'Billy.'"

"And laughed at him. I'd rather be taken seriously."

"Sure, Sheriff," said Mavis, thinking she'd do anything to keep Phoebe happy. "I hear Mom's having a party for you Saturday night."

"I was hoping she'd forget about that."

"Well, she didn't, so I guess we'll see you there. And I'll see you at the rally on Saturday."

Phoebe made a noncommittal noise and Mavis decided not to press her luck. Phoebe, even in uniform pants that were too long and even insisting on being called "sheriff," was a distinct improvement over Billy Benson. And Phoebe wouldn't stay mad at her long. She wasn't capable of carrying grudges.

As they left, Patsy said, "Cute office you have here, Phoebe," and Patty echoed, "Adorable." Mavis could have sworn she heard the Indian laugh.

"FRIENDS OF YOURS, SHERIFF?" asked Richie after the women had left the building.

"The one doing all the talking was my sister."

That hadn't been hard to figure out. Even in those godawful clothes and without any makeup at all, the woman had been a dead ringer for Katie Lou. And what a waste, a good-looking woman like that living with a bunch of crazies.

"You don't mind putting in some time on Saturday?" Phoebe inquired.

Richie not only didn't mind, since there wasn't much to do on weekends when Maggie didn't come home, he couldn't wait. He'd love to see the sheriff in action. "I don't mind," he said.

"You really think they need protection?"

"Well, there was a little trouble last time. No harm done, but some of the men in town heckled them. And I'm afraid our former sheriff was one of the hecklers." He could remember Billy, his face red, his fat hand gesturing with the ever present cigar, really giving it to the women.

"I see," said Phoebe. "Well, I don't want that to happen again."

"That's going to be a little hard to predict, Sheriff. The thing is, most of the men around here find that group... well, I guess you would say, objectionable."

He could see her bristle. "Objectionable? In what way?"

"You know what I mean, Sheriff."

"I'm afraid I don't. For a short while I lived in that commune, and those women were very kind and understanding to me and my children."

He wondered, for about the hundredth time, just how many children she had. He found himself thinking of that odd little house of hers, then of the nursery rhyme about the old woman who lived in a shoe.

But wait, hold on a moment. She had lived in that crazy commune, hadn't she? Well, she said she had, so what did that make her? Another crazy, that's what. And he figured he could pretty much write the scenario: husband and wife, children, everything going along smoothly. Then the wife, for whatever misguided reasons she might have had, takes the kids and ups and leaves the husband to become a part of the commune made up of the strangest women imaginable. It was a story he had heard before. Gone were the days when men left their wives; now it was the wives who were doing the leaving. And, in either case, it was the kids who did the suffering.

The sheriff might blush and she might come across as strictly feminine in the oddest moments, but the bottom line was, he was working for a woman who had no use for men.

It was going to take a little thinking about. But somehow, some way, he was going to have to find a way to dump this sheriff and put in office someone a normal man could tolerate taking orders from.

Then the sheriff was talking to him, saying, "That drifter my sister mentioned, the one camping out in the cemetery. Do you know anything about that?"

Richie nodded. "Billy went out to talk to him."

"What happened?"

"I don't know. He came back drunk and that was the last I heard of it."

"Well, why don't we check it out in the morning, unless something more important comes up, of course."

"Fine with me, Sheriff," said Richie, thinking it would break up the monotony. Billy's idea of a busy day had been getting in enough nap time. Plus he couldn't wait to see the new sheriff in action.

He was about to say something else, but just then the door to the office opened and in walked two kids.

And somehow, without even asking, Richie knew they weren't there on business.

Chapter Five

Ben snuggled up next to her in the car and whispered in her ear, "He looks like an Indian."

"Yes, he does," said Phoebe, remembering the way Ben had kept sneaking looks at Richie in the office.

"I like Indians," Ben declared.

Phoebe had always had a partiality for Indians herself. Not that she had ever actually met any. She was beginning to have a partiality for Richie, too, and she thought it had something to do with the fact that she was his boss.

He was the first man she hadn't felt she had to defer to. Not that he didn't know more about being a sheriff and she certainly would need to ask him questions and seek his advice on their work, but it was a totally different feeling when you were the boss. She had always looked up to her father and done what he'd said. Even in her marriage she had looked up to Ted and he'd always had the last word. But with Richie, she had the last word, even if it was the wrong word. And even though Richie didn't seem to appreciate it, she was enjoying it.

"I've got to say, Mother," said Dory, her bossy voice going into overdrive, "I think your behavior is most unprofessional."

Phoebe waited with bated breath to hear what was coming next. Her daughter had appointed herself arbiter of her mother's behavior ever since the divorce.

"Are you listening to me?" Dory demanded to know.

"Yes, of course, darling."

The use of the word "darling" did nothing to soften Dory's tone. "I'll take it in order of sequence. First of all, Mother, there's the matter of your being late for work."

"Oh, I really don't think that matters. After all, I'm the boss."

"And as such, you should set a good example. What would you think if our teachers were always late to school? And who would provide the discipline if they were?"

"I think you're overreacting, Dory. I've only been late one day."

"You've only gone to work one day. I know you, Mother. I know how you like to sleep in the morning."

"Perhaps you should wake me, then. You know how I always sleep through the alarm."

"I'd be glad to," said Dory. "Then there's the matter of your children showing up after school. I really don't think our place is in the office with you."

"I liked it there," said Ben, who had spent most of his time being instructed on the CB radio by Richie.

"I'm not going to leave you alone after school," Phoebe said. Plus she had enjoyed their being there. It had made the office seem like a home away from

Phoebe's Deputy

home, gave it a cozy feeling that it didn't have when it was just her and Richie.

"If I told you I got a job baby-sitting after school, you wouldn't object. So why should you object if I'm home alone with Ben for an hour?"

"We don't even have a phone in case of an emergency."

"I can use a neighbor's phone."

Dory's logic was often tiring. It also reminded Phoebe of the way Mavis had been as a child. Not that Dory was really like Mavis, thank heavens, but she didn't want her to be even a little like her. As a child Phoebe had always known that she was her mother's favorite and Mavis was her father's, and she had sworn she wouldn't have favorites when she had her own children. But even though she loved them both beyond reason, it was far more satisfying to cuddle up with Ben than it was to argue with her daughter. "Anything else, Dory?"

"No. Well, I did hear about your use of the siren this morning. Everyone was talking about it."

"That was an accident. I didn't know how to turn it off."

"I'll show you," said Ben, and the next thing she knew, the siren was blaring again and the cars in front of her were scattering.

RICHIE SMILED ACROSS THE BAR at Katie Lou. "Funny thing, Katie Lou," he said to her, "a couple of days ago I hadn't even known you were ever married. Now I've met two of your daughters and two of your grandkids. And may I say, you're sure not my idea of a grandmother."

Rather than looking pleased by the compliment, Katie Lou got a proud gleam in her eyes. "Then you've met them all, Richie. That's all I've got—two daughters and two grandchildren."

Richie got this urge to interrogate Katie Lou about at least one of her daughters, but then he thought how miffed he'd be if someone went to see his mother and started questioning her about him. Still, he didn't have to actually ask questions. He could just kind of make a few statements and wait for Katie Lou to pick up the ball and run with it.

Richie looked down the bar to where Billy Benson was sitting, drowning his sorrows. He'd nodded to Billy when he came in, but hadn't bothered to start up a conversation with him. Billy looked too drunk to string a sentence together. Lowering his voice, he said, "Kind of strange having a woman sheriff."

"I can imagine," said Katie Lou. "Rather like having a female bartender, I expect."

Richie didn't think it was the same at all. Being a bartender was rather like being a waitress. A female sheriff, on the other hand, was like Wyatt Earp getting a sex change.

"That one daughter of yours, she's the image of you."

"That would be Mavis. She looks like me, but she has her father's mind."

Richie didn't know quite what to make of that remark unless Katie Lou's husband had been crazy. He had time to think about it, though, because one of the state troopers had come in. He took a seat next to Richie and ordered coffee, which Richie figured meant he was either on duty or going on soon.

"What do you say, Richie?" said Frank, then turned his attention to Katie Lou. "How're you holding up, Katie, luv?"

Richie had heard that Frank had been seeing something of Katie Lou, but he had put it down to unfounded rumor until now. From Katie Lou's look of pleasure at Frank, though, he had to assume there was truth in it.

While Katie Lou was getting coffee for Frank, Frank turned to him and said, "How do you like your new boss? I stopped by there this morning when I got off duty, but she wasn't in yet."

"She was late to work," Richie said.

"You talking about Phoebe?" asked Katie Lou, and when Richie nodded, she said, "Phoebe has a habit of sleeping a lot when she's unhappy with life."

"If she's unhappy with being sheriff," Richie said, "she should just resign."

"Oh, that'll probably cross her mind," Katie Lou said. "But I have a feeling if she sticks it out, she'll find it'll be something she likes."

In that case, Richie hoped she wouldn't stick it out. Nothing personal, but he'd still like to be sheriff someday.

"She's got to be an improvement over Billy," Frank commented, just a shade too loudly.

Richie, who had been keeping an eye on him, saw Billy turn his head in their direction. "You boys talking about me?" asked the former sheriff.

"Just wondering how you were doing, Billy," Frank called down the bar.

"Go to hell," Billy grumbled.

Richie said to Frank, "What you just said, about how she had to be an improvement over Billy, I wouldn't be so sure. Course she's stayed sober so far...."

"That's not what I meant," said Frank. "What I meant, stupid, was that it must be a hell of a lot more fun working with a good-looking woman than with an old drunk."

"You think she's good-looking?" Richie asked. He thought so himself, but since he often was attracted to offbeat types, he wanted confirmation.

The confirmation, however, came from Katie Lou. "You think I'd go and have a daughter who wasn't good-looking?" she asked him.

"Did I say that, Katie Lou?" asked Richie.

"The fact is, Richie, she's one of the best women you'll ever meet. Maybe the best."

"You trying your hand at matchmaking?" Frank asked her.

"Not at all," Katie Lou said. "I just want Richie to know what he's missing out on, that's all."

"I hear you're throwing a party for her," said Richie.

"That's right." Katie Lou nodded. "Saturday night, and I expect you to be here."

Unfortunately Billy must have overheard that last bit of news, because just as Frank was leaning across the bar and saying, "Give me a kiss, Katie, luv," Richie saw movement out of the corner of his eyes, but by the time he turned it was too late.

Billy Benson had gotten off his barstool, then lifted it up and thrown it through the plant-filled picture window.

Billy had always prided himself on being a man of action.

Phoebe's Deputy

PHOEBE HAD TUCKED BEN into bed and read him the latest chapter in *Charlotte's Web*, one of Ben's favorite books. Now, as she bent to kiss him good-night, she said, "Do you mind my being sheriff, honey?"

"I don't mind. I like it. I got to be one of the good guys today, only I got shot anyway."

"It will mean I won't be here when you get home from school."

"But only for a little while."

"For about an hour. And during that time, Dory will be in charge."

"Dory will boss me around."

"That's right."

"I don't mind. Sometimes she plays games with me."

"I could resign, Ben. There's nothing saying I have to be sheriff if I don't feel like it."

"I think you should be sheriff, Mom. If you find out you really hate it and want to quit, I'll hide you under my bed, where they'll never find you."

"Thank you," she told him, taking the offer in the same seriousness in which it had been meant.

"Mom? How do spiders make their webs?"

"You've seen me knitting, haven't you, Ben?"

"Sure. You make me mittens."

"Well, that's what the spiders do. They knit."

"Really?"

"Maybe," said Phoebe.

When she went downstairs it was nine o'clock and Dory was reading the dictionary. She was afraid Dory was going to be an intellectual like Phoebe's father and sister. Already Dory knew more words than Phoebe did, which sometimes made her feel inadequate. Ted had been somewhat of an intellectual, but nothing like her dad and Mavis. In Phoebe's childhood Mavis and her father had always corrected her use of words at the dinner table, which had resulted in Phoebe's being particularly quiet during that meal.

"Are you going to bed soon?" she asked Dory.

"In a little while."

"I was thinking of going to bed myself. If I have to get up at seven..." She let the words trail off, not wanting any lectures from Dory about how she slept too much.

"Go ahead, then," Dory said.

"I'll wait till you're through in the bathroom."

Phoebe couldn't explain why, but she liked to know that Ben and Dory were asleep before she went to bed. She picked up her knitting—a pair of red mittens she was making for Ben—and remembered how she had hidden her knitting when she first went to live at the commune. She had been sure that the other women would think it was too feminine a thing to be doing. Instead she found that this particular group of feminists were into doing everything for themselves, from baking bread to weaving on a loom. Not Mavis, of course, but since all the others were doing similar things, she knew Mavis wouldn't be able to chide her for knitting.

Mavis was able to pay her share of the expenses at the commune by tutoring high school students. Mavis took great pride in the fact that she tutored for a living, which to Phoebe was an indication that Mavis thought of herself as understated. A Ph.D. from Harvard tutoring for a living seemed rather like the way rich people wore old jeans. Phoebe thought it was a waste of Mavis's education, but the one time she said something like that to her sister, she was told that's what men would say and she expected better from Phoebe. Phoebe never mentioned it again.

When the knock came at the door, Phoebe thought, speak of the devil, sure that it was Mavis on one of her late-night visits. Phoebe had been able to stand up to Mavis in her office, but now, at home, she knew she wouldn't have the advantage. She also wasn't wearing her uniform. For some reason, the minute she had put that uniform on, she had become ninety percent more assertive than she'd ever been before. It had surprised her as much as it had seemed to surprise Mavis.

"Want me to get that, Mom?" Dory asked.

"No, I'll get it," Phoebe said, carefully setting aside her knitting before getting up.

When she opened the door, though, it wasn't Mavis. Instead it was a state trooper.

"I'm Trooper Willis, Sheriff," he said, not for a moment betraying in any way that he might be surprised to see the sheriff wearing a pink fuzzy robe and armadillo slippers.

"How can I help you?" asked Phoebe, wondering if she should invite him in.

"There's a little trouble down at The Greenery. We thought maybe you could come down and help us out."

"My mother owns The Greenery."

"Yes, ma'am, I know. It was her idea that I come and get you. She said the sheriff is obliged to keep the peace and she's in need of your help."

"But our department's closed down at night."

"I'm aware of that, ma'am. It's just that it's the sheriff, or rather the ex-sheriff. Billy's gotten himself drunker than a skunk and is hell-bent on destroying The Greenery."

"Couldn't you stop him?" Phoebe asked.

"It's not that we can't stop him, Sheriff. It's more like your mother wants him arrested for drunk and disorderly and thrown into jail."

"Can't you do that?"

"We could, but no one will. You see, ma'am, most of us have worked with Billy at one time or another. None of us wants to throw him in jail. It's kind of a question of loyalty. He may not have been the greatest law enforcement officer, but he was one of us."

"I see. So I have to be the bad guy," Phoebe said, feeling very much as though she were in one of Ben's games.

"If you wouldn't mind, we'd sure appreciate it."

"No, I don't mind. Come in and have a seat while I change my clothes."

"You going out, Mom?" Dory asked.

"For a little while."

"That's okay. We'll be all right."

Maybe they'd be all right, Phoebe thought, but she wouldn't. Not only didn't she know how to arrest anyone, but she wouldn't get her nine hours' sleep, either.

BILLY HAD FINALLY run out of steam.

After demolishing the picture window and a few potted plants, destroying a few bottles and barstools and putting up a halfhearted fight with two of the troopers, he was now sitting on the floor, his back against the wall, his legs straight out in front of him and a mutinous look on his face. He was daring one and all to try to arrest him.

Richie couldn't wait to see what happened when the sheriff arrived. For openers, he was sure that Phoebe would blush when she heard the kind of language that had been emanating from Billy's mouth. Then she'd no doubt start in with a little feminist rhetoric picked up from her stay in the commune, the effect of which on Billy would probably be that he'd start tearing the place up again.

It should make for an interesting night.

But when Phoebe finally walked in the door, she didn't look militant at all. She looked nervous. She glanced over to where Billy was sitting on the floor, then to the group of troopers, among whom Richie was seated, at the end of the bar. She ended up walking over to Katie Lou.

"What's the matter, Mom?" she asked her.

"I want that man arrested and thrown into jail," said Katie Lou. "He thinks he can do damage to my bar with impunity just because he used to be sheriff. Someone needs to teach Billy Benson a lesson."

Phoebe looked over at the troopers. "She's made out a formal complaint, Sheriff," Richie called out.

"Then why hasn't anyone arrested him?" Phoebe asked.

Richie waited for one of the troopers on duty to speak, and when neither of them did, he said, "That'd be like asking you to arrest your mother, Sheriff."

"What started it?" Phoebe asked.

Richie shook his head. "I don't know. Your mother was telling us about the party she's having on Saturday night, and the next thing we knew Billy was breaking up the place."

Phoebe nodded, as though she understood something he didn't understand. She walked across the room to where Billy was sitting and, in a surprise move, sat down on the floor next to him. They looked to all the world like a couple of kids sitting there.

"What's the matter, Mr. Benson?" the sheriff asked him.

At first Billy just looked confused. He probably hadn't been called Mr. Benson in thirty years. But after a few seconds he mumbled, "It's Katie Lou." And then, even from a few yards away, Richie could have sworn he saw tears in Billy's eyes. Drunken tears to be sure, but still tears.

But what was even more surprising than Billy's tears was the sheriff's next move. She reached around Billy's shoulders with her arm and pulled him close to her. By God, she was acting like a mother!

Richie looked around and saw some raised eyebrows in the room. When he looked at Katie Lou, though, she was smiling. She caught Richie's eye and said, low enough not to be overheard by Phoebe, "That girl's a born mother."

"Tell me about it, Billy," said Phoebe, and he was damned if she didn't sound like a mother, too. He could imagine her using that exact same tone of voice with her little boy.

"I'm in love with that woman," Billy said, although his words weren't all that clear. "I'm in love with her, and she treats me like a swarm of blackflies."

There were some sounds of surprise around him and Richie figured he had made one of those sounds, too. It was the shock of the thing. He had been sure that Billy's rage had been directed at the new sheriff or the fact that he had lost the election. In the ten years he had known Billy he had never known him to be soft on a woman.

"You're in love with my mother?" Phoebe asked, looking for confirmation.

Billy nodded, and now the tears coming out of his bloodshot eyes were evident to everyone watching.

"My mother's a very good woman," said the sheriff in a soothing voice. "I'm sure she's always nice to you. She's nice to everyone."

"The man's a drunk," Katie Lou sang out.

Phoebe shot her mother a stern look, then turned back to Billy. Billy, starting to shake a little now, said, "See what I mean? She just called me a drunk."

"You do seem to be a little smashed," Phoebe observed.

Billy got a mulish look on his face. "Drunk or sober, it doesn't make any difference. She likes younger men."

"You're a fat, sloppy drunk, Billy Benson," said Katie Lou in a very clear voice. "I don't like fat, sloppy young drunks, either."

Billy's head was now slowly moving in the direction of the sheriff's shoulder. When it finally came to rest there, he was heard to mumble, "I know she's too good for me, but I can't help loving her, can I?"

Phoebe's other arm went around him and the next thing they knew she was practically rocking old Billy in her arms. She gave her mother a furious look and said, "Do you really want to see him locked up in a jail?"

Katie Lou appeared to be backing down. "I want to see him pay for the damage he did to my place," she said.

"Did you hear that, Billy?" Phoebe asked him. "Will you be willing to pay for the damage you did?"

Billy nodded, his fat face scrunched up in a way that made him look exactly like a Cabbage Patch Kid.

"Come on, then," said Phoebe, "I'm going to drive you home."

And while the occupants of The Greenery watched, the new sheriff pulled Billy Benson to his feet, then led him out the door.

A hushed silence followed. Then Katie Lou said, "She always did have a way with kids, and Billy acts like a big kid. Like the neighborhood bully."

There was general laughter and Richie ordered another beer. "I'm glad he didn't have to be locked up," he said. "I think that would just about have killed Billy."

"Maybe so," said Katie Lou, "but he can't go around thinking he's above the law."

"That was news to me he's in love with you," Frank said, sounding a little miffed about the whole thing.

"It was news to me, too, but I guess I should've seen it," Katie Lou said. "I just thought he hung out here all the time because he was a drunk."

Richie stood up and threw some money on the bar. "I think I'll drive by Billy's place, make sure she got him home all right."

He could see he scored points with Katie Lou for that one, but Frank muttered, "Looking to move in on her, Richie?"

"Maggie's about all I can handle," said Richie, but it didn't mean much, because Maggie was never around anymore and everyone in the bar knew it.

He just wanted to make sure that no one thought he was going after the new sheriff. That might be Frank's style, but it wasn't his. He was afraid that Billy might have had a change of heart on the way home and maybe be giving the sheriff a hard time. And Richie didn't think she'd be able to handle Billy at his worst.

PHOEBE HAD PULLED into Billy's driveway and was having a cigarette with him before helping him to the door. Billy had been silent all the way home, but now he said, "I appreciate what you did for me."

"I didn't do anything," said Phoebe.

"Saved my pride, that's what you did. I went and acted like a damn fool, deserved to get myself thrown in jail."

"I imagine you resent my taking your job because of a technicality."

Billy slid down a little in the seat. "That wasn't no technicality, ma'am. Only I'd appreciate it if you didn't tell anyone, particularly Richie."

"You mean you purposely didn't file?"

He nodded. "I've had enough of being sheriff, figured it was time to get out. But I knew if I told anyone, I'd get a big argument over it."

"What'll you do now?" Phoebe asked, hoping he wasn't going to drink full time now that he didn't have a job.

"I had this idea, but Katie Lou shot it all full of holes tonight. I guess I should've known better. A woman like her wouldn't see anything in someone like me."

"Mom's enjoying her independence," Phoebe said, realizing at that moment that it was true. Phoebe only wished she enjoyed hers.

"Richie probably isn't taking well to working for a female," Billy said. As he said it, a car pulled up in front of Billy's house and Billy turned around and squinted at it. "That's Richie now. I guess he's keeping an eye on you."

"I've gathered he doesn't like working for a woman," said Phoebe, thinking what a shame it was for Richie that Billy hadn't told Richie he didn't want to be sheriff anymore. If he had told him, Richie would be sheriff now, not her.

"Well, you can't altogether fault him for that," Billy said, sounding more sober by the minute. "He'd have made a good sheriff himself. Probably resents some woman with no experience coming in as his boss."

"Which was your fault, not mine."

"I know that. And I regret it in a way, too. In another way, though, now that I've met you, maybe I did the right thing. You might bring something new to law enforcement—compassion."

"Thanks, Billy." Phoebe smiled, putting out her cigarette and reaching for the door handle. "I guess I better be getting home, but I'll see you to the door."

"I'm okay now. And it's me who should thank you, and I truly do."

She stayed in the driveway while he walked to the door, and when she saw that his walk was now steady, she put the car in reverse and backed out of the driveway. She gave a wave to Richie to show him she was all right, then headed for home.

Instead of him going on his way, though, she saw him make a U-turn and follow her. When he didn't turn off anywhere and was still behind her when she reached her house, she began to be annoyed. Did he think the sheriff couldn't find her own way home? That she needed protecting?

She locked up her official car and walked back to where Richie was parked a few yards behind her. When he rolled down his window, she said, "There was no need to follow me."

"I just wanted to see how you made out with Billy. Did he give you any trouble?"

"I think if you treat people with respect, they'll respond with the same," Phoebe replied.

Richie chuckled. "Is that what you call it? Respect? It appeared to me that you were treating Billy like a child."

Phoebe could feel the blush, but luckily it wouldn't be noticeable in the dark. "Was I really?"

Richie nodded. "You were talking to him the same way you were talking to that son of yours in the office today."

"Oh, dear."

"Hey, I'm not knocking it. It seemed to do the trick with Billy. I'd hate to see you try something like that on a hardened criminal, though."

Richie was being so friendly she thought maybe she could clear the air a little between them. "Billy said you would resent working for a female. Is that true?"

He stared at her for a moment, then lowered his eyes. "I guess some men might feel that way."

"Do you?"

"Well, I do and I don't. It'd help, though, if you would take it more seriously. So far you've seemed more interested in interior decoration and buying yourself some new clothes than in learning what the job's all about."

Phoebe, who loved her new clothes and the way the office now looked, felt immediate guilt. "I suppose you mean learning how to shoot a gun."

"No, there's more to it than that. Although I would say it's pretty hard to be a law officer when you're a firm advocate of no guns."

Phoebe, who had never been a firm advocate of anything, decided, on second thought, that maybe she was. And yet she knew that if anyone was threatening her children, she'd use a gun or whatever else she could lay her hands on to protect them. Which started her thinking that as sheriff, she was responsible for the safety of all the children in the county. "Would you teach me how to use one?" she asked him.

He smiled. "Be glad to. All you've got to do is ask and I'll teach you anything you want to learn." He reached out a hand and gently pinched her nose. "You're freezing standing out there. If you want to continue the conversation, why don't you get in the car?"

Just the quick touch of his fingers on her nose had been enough to make her jump. "Oh, thank you, but, no, I don't think I'd better. It's late, much later than I thought, and if I don't go in now I'll never get up on time in the morning." And she had a feeling that if she got into his car she might want to be touched again.

She heard his chuckle. "Well, we wouldn't want that, would we? Okay, Sheriff, have a good night's sleep and I'll see you in the morning."

He had been laughing at her, she knew. She had reacted to his first show of friendliness by acting like a skittish teenager. He was just being nice and polite and considerate and she had reacted as though he had some ulterior motive for inviting her into his car. Like making out. As though he were even interested in her, which was about as remote a possibility as it was possible for her to think of. Interested in her? As a woman? Good heavens, about the last person a good-looking man like Richie would be interested in would be a skinny divorced woman with two kids.

He could even be married. But would a married man be hanging around The Greenery at night? Alone? Well, maybe. It was always possible.

The thing was, she had been dying to get into his car. The whole time they had talked she had been thinking how warm and cozy it would be to be inside the car with Richie. She was a disgrace to her badge; there was no other word for it. While he was acting in a professional manner, she had been daydreaming about getting close to the first man who had appealed to her since her husband.

There were things about Richie that were so nice. Like the way he'd been with Ben and Dory. Of course, Ben, with his lovable ways, was always a favorite with adults, but Richie had given some attention to Dory, too, and Dory had responded with more warmth than she usually showed to strangers.

She found herself thinking that if she and Richie were ever to marry, their children might look like red-haired Indians. Not that Dory and Ben had red hair; they had both inherited their father's brown hair and hazel eyes. That hadn't really surprised Phoebe, because Ted had always had his way in everything. Besides, she wouldn't have wanted them to have red hair anyway. Children always make jokes about other children with red hair. At least they had been spared that.

Marrying Richie was a very silly thing to be thinking about anyway. A man that age would've been married by now if he was so inclined. Besides, she didn't want to get married again. Once she had thought that marriages were forever, but now that she knew they weren't, she didn't think she'd risk it again. She had her children, which had been the best part of marriage anyway.

It certainly hadn't been the sex. In fact, sex had been a great disappointment to her. She had always imagined it would be the most thrilling experience of her life, but it hadn't been like that at all. At first it had taken some getting used to, and then, when she finally thought she was getting good at it and it was beginning to look as though it might turn thrilling at any moment, Ted had begun to lose interest in making love. Of course, in retrospect, he might have had girlfriends even then. At the time she had attributed his disinterest to the fact that she was spending more time with the children than with him.

It wouldn't do to start getting interested in a man who would likely as not break her heart the way Ted had done. She should just accept him as what he was, an interesting man she would be working with. With luck they could become friends, and a friend was something she could use a lot more than she could use another husband.

The thing was, she knew how her mind worked. She was a romantic, there was no getting around it, and it was going to be awfully hard not to romanticize what could be instead of being practical over what really was.

Maybe she should have stayed in the commune. There were temptations out here she hadn't even dreamed of.

Chapter Six

The cemetery was a pristine white. Gravestones loomed up like substantial ghosts as Phoebe and Richie trudged through the snow. The tent, which they could see in the distance, was inconveniently placed on the very farthest edge of the graveyard.

Phoebe couldn't tell the bushes from the gravestones and got more than one bruise because of a wrong guess. Richie was following her, and if she thought she heard a few subdued chuckles when her shin would hit something hard, she ignored them. She had insisted on taking the lead; she would now suffer the consequences.

For some reason she had pictured the tent as being white, despite the fact that she had seen enough tents sold in sporting goods stores to know they were never white. This one was green—the only bit of green in the entire landscape.

She wondered what kind of an idiot would choose to live outdoors in a tent during a Vermont winter. She found enduring a Vermont winter difficult enough in a house. He would have to be a drunk. Only a drunk, his veins filled with alcohol, would manage not to freeze to death in temperatures—even without the windchill factor—that rarely rose above freezing.

Even though her khaki pants were shoved into her boots, they weren't surviving the snow well. In fact, they were quickly soaked through to above the knees. Even the long underwear she wore beneath the pants appeared to be soaked. A quick glance behind her told her that Richie wasn't suffering the same problem. He was using her footprints to step into, making his walk much easier. And drier.

The closer she got to the tent the larger it appeared. She found she rather liked the looks of that one piece of greenery amid all the blinding white. It was restful to keep her eyes on the tent. Somehow it didn't look like the tent of a crazy person; it looked more like a tent that was meant for a milder clime but had been misplaced.

When she was ten yards from the tent, she heard a distinct click behind her and she stopped dead in her tracks. Looking behind her, she saw her intrepid deputy, gun in hand.

"Put that away this minute," she ordered him, hearing too late that she sounded exactly the way she did when she told Ben to put away his toys.

"It's standard operating procedure, Sheriff," Richie said, sounding much the way Ben did when he was giving her excuses for why his toys had to remain exactly in place.

She turned around to face him. "Are you telling me that there's a rule written down that says you must draw your gun when approaching a tent?"

"We don't know who might be inside it, Sheriff."

"We know it's someone who was hospitable to Sheriff Benson," she reminded him. "Anyway, it's making me nervous, so kindly put it out of sight. If you're afraid to approach the tent without a gun, I'll go by myself."

The gun was returned to its holster.

Phoebe didn't know the proper way to make her presence known to an inhabitant of a tent. There was no doorbell, no door to knock on, and their footsteps made no sound in the snow that might herald their arrival. If there was someone inside and he had heard their voices, he wasn't coming out to greet them.

She cleared her throat and felt a little silly when she called out, "It's the Sheriff. Please open up."

She felt even sillier when she heard the muffled laughter behind her, then Richie said, "You don't need to say 'please,' Sheriff. This isn't exactly a social call."

Phoebe saw no reason why law enforcement officials shouldn't show the same good manners as other people. Still, when it didn't get a response, she raised her voice and shouted, "Is anyone home?"

She heard the sound of a zipper being unzipped, then the flap was lifted and a small, lightly clad man with the face of an elf looked out. "A gorgeous redhead. Just what I was hoping for," he said, ignoring Richie behind her.

Phoebe looked down to see if her badge was in place. It was. "We've had a complaint about you, sir—"

"About me?" His smile was blinding. "Who would complain about me? I don't have a TV, no loud radio, and so far I haven't thrown even one wild party. Could I be told the nature of the complaint?"

Phoebe liked him instantly, and it was all she could do to keep from smiling. "It's against the law, sir, to camp out on private property. Unless, of course, you have permission."

"This is my property," he told her, and she was sorry to hear that. She had been sure he wasn't crazy, after all.

"Come on inside," he was saying. "I'll fix you a cup of tea."

Phoebe looked around at Richie.

"Go on," said Richie, "make your social call. I'll wait out here for you."

She glared at him before turning back to the man. "This really isn't a social call," she told him. "I'm afraid I'm going to have to evict you from this property."

The man looked past her to Richie. "Why don't both of you come in and warm up while we settle this?"

He stepped aside and Phoebe waited for Richie to enter first. When she entered the tent the air was warmer inside, and she couldn't figure out why, unless it was just being out of the wind.

The inside of the tent appealed very much to her nesting instinct. There was a warmly colored braided rug on the floor, maple bookcases filled with books, a maple desk and chair, a cot with a sleeping bag on top of it and large pillows scattered around the floor. In addition to the light coming in two plastic windows, three Coleman battery-operated lanterns were lit, giving the room a cheery look.

The elf was on the floor, putting some water on to boil at his camping stove. Phoebe selected one of the pillows and lowered herself to the ground. Richie, having to stoop slightly, remained standing.

The man turned his head around to look at her. "All I have is Lipton. I hope that's all right. I'm Noggie, by the way."

Phoebe thought that "noggie" sounded like slang for crazy, or maybe tired. It was a word she couldn't remember hearing before. "Noggie? What does that mean?" she asked him.

He grinned. "It doesn't mean anything. It's my name. It's Albert Noggie, but everyone just calls me Noggie. Except my mother, who has always insisted on calling me Bert, and my father, who rather favored Al. Are you a policewoman?"

"I'm Sheriff Tripp," she told him, "and this is Deputy Stuart."

Noggie turned all the way around and sat crosslegged, facing her. "A lovely redheaded sheriff—how delightful! I knew I was right in moving here."

Phoebe felt herself blushing but was sure it wouldn't be noticed, as her face must already be pink from the cold. "I'm afraid there's been a complaint about your camping out on private property."

Noggie looked delighted. "But you see, it's my private property. I happen to be pitching tent on my portion of the family plot. If you'd care to go outside and brush some of the snow away, you'd see that my paternal grandparents are to the west of me and Uncle Joshua directly to the north. My tent is over the exact spot where I will someday rest in peace."

"I've never heard of anybody doing something like that," Phoebe said, not having a clue about where the law stood on this.

"I don't see why I shouldn't," Noggie said. "It happens to be the only land I own, so I didn't see why I had to wait until I was dead to begin enjoying it. My tent's not an eyesore, is it? As soon as spring thaw arrives—if it ever does—I plan on putting in a garden."

Phoebe turned around to see what reaction this was having on Richie. He appeared to be halfway between intrigued and amused. She wanted to ask him if Noggie was breaking any laws, but didn't want to appear ignorant in her role as sheriff. Instead she said, "Why don't you sit down, Richie?"

With a smile in Noggie's direction, Richie took a seat on one of the pillows.

Phoebe continued, "I've also had a complaint from the women whose farm adjoins the cemetery. They say you're spying on them."

Noggie nodded his head. "Do you believe in ghosts?"

Phoebe heard a chuckle from Richie as she said, "No, I really don't."

"Neither do I," said Noggie, "but still, I thought if there were any, I'd surely see them here. Since I haven't seen a single ghost, and there's not much else to look at with everything covered with snow, I do spend some time watching those women. It's not quite as good as watching television, since it's only pictures with no sound, but since I don't have electricity, they're better than nothing. Why is it all I ever see are women? Are there no men on that farm?"

"It's a bunch of crazy feminists," said Richie.

"It is not," she corrected him, "it's the Crazy Quilt Women's Commune."

"That explains it," Noggie said, shifting his body back around to the stove as the water began to boil. He poured them each a cup of tea, adding sugar where it was asked for, then handed the cups around. After everyone had tasted the tea, Noggie said, "Inform the feminists that I am one of them. They have nothing to fear from me."

"One of them?" Richie's disbelief was obvious.

"Absolutely." Noggie's eyes positively danced with glee. "As a small man, I've learned a little bit about what the weaker sex has to go through in life."

"And what is that?" Richie asked.

"You wouldn't have to ask if you were small. For one thing, people tend to treat you like a child."

Richie chuckled. "I don't know about that. It was only last night that I saw quite a large man being treated like a child."

"There are always exceptions," Noggie said, "but I think you will find, generally speaking, that women and small people aren't taken seriously. Did you know that there was a time in history when royalty and the rich collected dwarfs? They were kept in much the same way we keep house pets these days."

"I don't believe you are a dwarf, sir," Richie said, his amusement showing.

"If I were a few inches shorter and less perfectly proportioned, you wouldn't be saying that," Noggie said.

"I'm afraid," said Phoebe, "that dwarfs are getting a little off the subject." Looking to Richie for confirmation, she continued, "I think that this is an area of the country where people make allowances for different life-styles. As far as I know the only complaint we've had about you camping out here has been from the commune. If we could come to some sort of peaceful compromise, I don't think it would be necessary to ask you to move." She stood up and walked over to one of the two windows. As she had surmised, it overlooked the commune. "If you would move your tent so that you couldn't see into the commune, I think the women would withdraw their complaint."

Noggie beamed at her. "You're very good at coming up with compromises, aren't you?"

Phoebe beamed back at him.

"The only problem is," Noggie said, "that you'd be depriving me of my entertainment. If I had a house situated here I'd be able to look out my windows, or gaze over the fence."

"They feel it's an invasion of their privacy," Phoebe explained, her beam having faded.

"That's utter nonsense," Noggie scoffed. "It's not as though I creep up to their house and peek through the windows. I can only see them when they're out of doors, just as anyone driving by could see them. Could it be that it's those dances they do in the moonlight that they object to my watching?"

"Dances?" Richie asked.

"Just an ancient custom they've revived," Phoebe said.

"You're familiar with it?" Noggie asked.

Blushing furiously, Phoebe said, "My sister lives there, as did I for a short time. They're rather private women, you see—"

"Private!" Richie exclaimed. "What about the rally they're holding tomorrow in the middle of town?"

"A rally?" Noggie asked. "I think I'd like to see that."

Feeling far more confused than a sheriff in this situation should feel, Phoebe set down her cup and got to her feet. "Perhaps you could talk to them yourself tomorrow, maybe come to your own compromise," she suggested.

"I'll certainly talk to them," Noggie said. "After watching them for so long it will be interesting to hear what their voices sound like."

Richie also got to his feet. "We'll see you there, then, Noggie. It ought to be interesting. There's a party tomorrow night at The Greenery, too. You should come and meet some of the locals."

"I'd like that. I imagine some of them must have relatives buried here, and I think it's always nice to know something about one's neighbors."

"I DON'T GET IT," Phoebe said, starting up the car. "First you want to go in there with a drawn gun, then you invite him to the party."

"I liked him."

"I liked him, too. Is he breaking the law?"

"I don't really know, Sheriff. Before we talked to him I figured he was trespassing on private property, but if he owns that plot of land, then I'm not sure. No invasion of privacy charge would stick, though, not if all he's doing is looking over a fence. Hell, I do that all the time."

Phoebe nodded in agreement. "I ought to stop by the commune and tell them."

"Let's do it."

"I'd rather not. I'm sure they'll think I wasn't doing my job."

"You afraid of those women, Sheriff?"

"No, of course not, why should I be afraid of them?"

"Then let's stop by."

"Well, I'm a little afraid of my sister."

Richie looked over at her with a grin. "You're kidding? Why would you be afraid of her? You're twice her size."

"It has nothing to do with size. I've always found her intimidating, that's all."

"Is she older than you?"

Phoebe nodded. "Two years."

"Well, Sheriff, two years might seem like a big difference when you're kids, but now that you're adults... I can't imagine being intimidated by anyone in my own family."

"They all intimidated me in one way or another. I don't think it was their fault, though. I think it was mine. I even let my daughter intimidate me at times."

Richie reached over so that his hands were on her shoulders. She immediately stiffened, but if he noticed it, it didn't show on his face. "Listen to me, Phoebe," he said, using her name for the first time. "You're the sheriff—the law in this county—and you shouldn't let anyone intimidate you. We're going over there right now and you're going to stand up to that sister of yours and get into a little intimidation yourself if need be."

"You called me 'Phoebe.'"

"Did you hear what I said?"

Phoebe smiled. "I heard. You'll come with me?"

"I wouldn't miss it, Sheriff."

"The thing is, we'll have to do it standing at the door. They don't allow males inside."

"Why not?"

"Don't ask me, Richie. I don't see that it makes any difference, because most of them sneak out to see men anyway."

"Even your sister?"

"Well, no, not Mavis. But she's the exception."

She pulled onto the road and headed for the commune. She had stood up to Mavis yesterday; there was no reason she couldn't stand up to her today. Except that she had had the advantage yesterday. She had known very well that Mavis was expecting her to be upset about winning the election; otherwise she would have come to see her with both guns blazing.

Well, now she'd have to stand up to her because Richie was expecting it. She could hardly knuckle under to one of the citizenry with her deputy along to watch.

"And don't blush," Richie advised her.

"What?"

"Don't let her make you blush. That's a sure sign of weakness."

"It's not something I can control, you know. And it isn't weakness—it's usually embarrassment."

"Well, don't let her embarrass you. You have nothing to be embarrassed about. You went into action today for the first time and you did just fine."

"That wasn't my idea of action."

"Well, we don't get anything too exciting around here."

Phoebe pulled up in front of the commune and parked. "I could always wait until tomorrow to tell her."

"One thing a sheriff never is, Phoebe, is chicken."

Phoebe could feel herself starting to blush, turned and saw that Richie had noticed, and they both began to laugh.

"What could I possibly have said to embarrass you?"

"Nothing. Nothing at all. Sometimes I don't even need a reason."

MAVIS AND THE OTHER MEMBERS of the Crazy Quilt Women's Commune had been watching all the action out of the windows.

Peggy had been the one to spot the sheriff's car go by and had alerted the others. They had all run to the back of the house and watched through the kitchen window, the only window in the house that afforded a perfect view of the tent.

They had seen Phoebe and her deputy pick their way slowly through the cemetery, then disappear into the green tent. While they waited for them to reappear, they had cups of herbal tea.

Then they had run back to the front room, where they could watch out the window for the sheriff's car to pass on its way back to town. When it didn't pass, when, instead, it stopped in front of their property, Mavis felt jubilant.

"You see?" she said to the others. "It's just as I said. Now that Phoebe's sheriff, people aren't going to hassle us anymore. I'll bet that drifter will be out of there by morning."

"Maybe she'll give him until Monday," Marian said. "Your sister has a good heart."

"Why're they sitting in the car?" Patsy asked.

"She's probably explaining to him that he'll have to wait in the car," Mavis said, but just then she saw both of them getting out.

"She's bringing him along," Deborah observed, a tiny note of excitement in her voice.

"She knows better than that," Peggy said.

"She's just acting professionally," Mavis explained. "We'll talk to them at the door, that's all."

"Maybe we could make an exception," Deborah said.

Mavis turned a quelling look on her. "An exception? You know what happens when you start making exceptions?"

Deborah shook her head, her entire body quivering.

"Principles go down the drain, that's what!"

Mavis waited for the knock at the door, then went ahead of the others to answer it. She had seen her in uniform just the day before, but still, it was a shock to see Phoebe standing there looking so official, her hat making her look a good foot taller than Mavis.

"So what happened?" Mavis asked. "Did you throw him out?"

She could have sworn Phoebe looked smug when she said, "Mr. Noggie hasn't broken any laws, Mavis. The plot of land he's camping on is his own."

"That's absolutely crazy! Any land inside that fence belongs to the cemetery."

"Yes, but it's his own plot."

Mavis glared up at her sister. "Unless I'm mistaken, Sheriff," she said, throwing tons of sarcasm into the word, "Mr. Noggie, if that's his name, is not dead. Correct me if I'm wrong, but since when are live people allowed to live in cemeteries?"

Phoebe seemed to shrink just a bit as she looked at her deputy. He in turn said, "We'll look up the statutes to see if there's any law on the books forbidding it, but as far as I know, he's not breaking any laws."

"Maybe Indians are allowed to reside in burial grounds," Mavis retorted, "but that isn't the way the rest of us do things."

"Indians?" asked the deputy.

"Aren't you an Indian?"

Phoebe interrupted. "This is Richie Stuart, Mavis, and he says he isn't Indian."

"I not only say it," said Richie, "it's the truth."

"Nobody cares whether you're an Indian or not," Mavis said, "the point is, what that man is doing can't be allowed. Do you really think, Phoebe, that Mother could move back to Princeton and build a house next to Dad's grave? Or is it just in Vermont that these things are permitted?"

"Richie already told you we'd look it up. We would certainly not move to evict him until we knew what the law was. Incidentally, Mavis, he's a feminist."

"I beg your pardon?"

"Mr. Noggie. He's a feminist."

"And I'm the queen of England!" Mavis slammed the door in her sister's face.

"That was rude, Mavis," Deborah said.

"She's not going to be any help at all."

"She tried," Peggy said, "and I think she did very well considering she's only been sheriff for three days."

"If she doesn't help us," Mavis said, "we'll have to think of a solution ourselves."

"We could plant some trees along our side of the fence," suggested Patsy.

"Which would take twenty years to grow big enough to block his view." Mavis shook her head.

"We could build a wall," Marian offered.

"What kind of a wall?" asked Mavis.

"You know, like the Berlin Wall. Or the Great Wall of China. Something that would completely blot him out of our landscape."

"How do you build a wall when we're hip deep in snow?" Mavis wanted to know.

"We build it of snow."

Mavis thought it was a silly, inept idea, particularly since they were due for a thaw any day now, which would melt the wall. The others, though, seemed excited about the idea and were already getting into boots and mittens and acting as though building a wall were an adventure.

Forget a wall. What would really give her pleasure would be to pelt that damn tent with a few well-aimed snowballs.

As for her sister the sheriff, Mavis hadn't liked the glances she had seen exchanged between Phoebe and that Indian look-alike. She had looked interested in him, the way women looked when they were interested in men. That was something she definitely didn't want to see. Phoebe interested in a man meant Phoebe interested in getting married again, which meant Phoebe wanting more babies, and then where would they be? Back with a man for a sheriff, that's where.

What's more, the deputy had been looking at Phoebe in exactly the same way.

Mavis thought Phoebe had learned her lesson when Ted had left her. And she had been sure that lesson had been reinforced during her stay at the commune.

Now she'd have to reassess that thinking and come up with a plan. Phoebe must not be allowed to go that route again, and Mavis was the only one to save her.

WHEN BEN GOT HOME from school the black cat was sitting on the front porch. Ben could tell the cat had been waiting for him, as the cat's ears went back as soon as Ben approached, and as Ben went up the steps, the cat quickly started to wash his back, as though he were getting ready to be taken into the house and wanted to be good and clean.

Ben had never had it happen before that a cat sought him out rather than the other way around. "Good cat," he said, reaching down and patting the top of his head. The cat quickly bit his hand, but it wasn't a hard bite at all. It left teeth marks, but there wasn't any blood. Then, after he bit him, the cat washed with his tongue the part of Ben's hand that he had bitten.

Ben opened the door with his key, and without even having to pick up the cat, the cat walked right by him into the house and headed straight for the kitchen.

Before he even took off his jacket, Ben poured the cat a bowl of milk and a glass for himself. He had been right, the cat did want to live with him, only no one was going to believe him. Finally he could say that a cat had followed him home and it would be the truth, except all the other times he had said the same thing, and now that it really had happened, Mom and Dory would think he was lying.

If only the cat would stay upstairs out of sight, maybe it would be okay. But cats never did what you wanted them to do. They went wherever they liked and there was no way to stop them.

By the time Dory got home a few minutes later the cat had decided that what he liked was the couch, and he was stretched out on it, taking up two of the three cushions. He was purring and washing his paws and

Phoebe's Deputy

seemed right at home. Ben was sitting on the third cushion and trying to think of some way to talk his mom into letting him keep the cat.

Dory came in holding some mail in her hand, and as soon as she saw the cat she said, "That looks like the same cat."

"It is," Ben said.

"Followed you home again, right?"

"He was on the porch when I got home. He really was, Dory. I'm not lying."

Dory didn't seem to be listening to him, though. Instead she sat down in the rocking chair and was opening one of the envelopes.

"You shouldn't open Mom's mail," Ben said.

"It's not for Mom—it's for me. From Dad."

"Dad wrote to you?" Ben hadn't heard from or seen his dad since the divorce.

"I wrote to him first. I wasn't sure he would know where we were."

"What'd you say to him, Dory?"

"I just told him about the house Mom had gotten us and about school and things. The letter's to both of us. Do you want to hear it?"

Ben nodded, too surprised to speak. He had never thought he could just write his father a letter and his father would write back.

"'Dear kids,'" she read, "'I tried to get a phone number for you so that I could talk to you, but your mother doesn't appear to be listed up there. I miss you both and I hope you're behaving yourselves. I live in an apartment now near the university, and if you come to visit me I have a couch that makes into a bed, but you'll have to share it.'"

"What's an apartment?" Ben asked.

"You know what apartments are, Ben."

"I forget."

"It's a building where a lot of people live and it doesn't have a yard."

"Go on, read the rest."

"'I'm married now, as you probably heard. We both like to ski and we'll be up in Stowe during spring break and I'll stop by and see you. Tell your mom I'd like to take you out for the day and you can pick out some place where you'd like to eat or something you might like to do. I love you both very much and I hope you haven't forgotten that I'm your father. Love, Dad.'"

"I didn't know he was married," Ben said.

"That's why he left us, because he wanted to marry someone else," Dory explained.

"Are you going to show Mom the letter?"

Dory folded it and put it into the pocket of her jeans. "I don't think so. I don't like to see her cry."

"It's scary when she cries."

"I just sent the letter to the university. I wasn't sure he'd get it."

"Are you going to write him back, Dory? Could I write something, too?"

"It'll be spring break in a couple of weeks, Ben. Why don't we wait until we've seen him?"

Ben nodded. He didn't know what he'd write anyway. He could say he missed him, because he did, but he didn't know if he'd say he loved him, because maybe he wasn't supposed to love him now that he was married to someone else.

"Who did he marry, Dory?"

"A student of his."

"Who told you?"

"No one told me. I heard Mom and Aunt Mavis talking about it. Aunt Mavis said you couldn't trust men."

"Aunt Mavis always says that." But he was going to be a man when he grew up. Did that mean no one would be able to trust him? Maybe it was because men lied, the way he had lied sometimes and said a cat had followed him home, when really he had picked up the cat and carried him home. He was sure that Mavis lied sometimes, too, only no one caught her at it.

"Don't mention the letter to Mom," Dory said. "She seems happier lately and I wouldn't want to upset her."

"She's happy because she has a new car and works with an Indian."

"He's not an Indian, Ben."

"I think he is. I think he's a secret Indian. He has to keep it a secret because lots of people kill Indians."

"Not anymore. That was a long time ago in history."

"Can Mom get married again if she wants to?"

"Sure, I suppose so."

"Would she be allowed to marry an Indian?"

"He's *not* an Indian, Ben."

Ben didn't know whether he wanted his mother to get married again anyway. If she got married again maybe she'd love her new husband more than she loved him. But maybe the new husband would play with Ben, and he would like that. He liked Richie even if he wasn't an Indian, because he talked to him as though he were a friend and not the way adults usually talked to him. He would like it better if he were an Indian, though. Then he'd be able to tell all his friends that his mother was married to an Indian, and they'd all think he was very lucky.

"Are we going to go somewhere with Dad when he comes here?"

"There's nowhere to go," Dory said. "I guess we could go to a restaurant."

"Maybe he would take us to Burlington to a movie." His mom had taken them a couple of times before it started to snow.

"That's probably a good idea, since I doubt whether Mom will want him around here."

"He doesn't want to see Mom? Just us?"

"He might bring his new wife. If he does, I don't think he'll want to see Mom. And if he sees her, she'll probably just cry."

Maybe his father would see Richie with his mom, and when Dad saw that Mom was friends with an Indian, he'd be so jealous he would want to come back and live with them. He didn't say this to Dory, though, because he was pretty sure that Dory would say that was silly. Maybe it was silly, but he wished something would make his dad come back and live with them again.

Maybe when his father saw Dory and him again he would realize he had made a mistake. Sometimes adults made mistakes, but when they did they hardly ever admitted it.

"Don't cry, Ben. It won't do any good."

"I'm not crying, Dory." But he bent his face so that he was hidden by the cat. The cat didn't even bite him; he just purred even louder.

Chapter Seven

Richie was glad for a reason to go to town.

He didn't like weekends when Maggie stayed on campus. Funny, when he was a kid, still in school, weekends were the only part of the week he really enjoyed. He was aware that most people he knew felt that way still, but not him. He preferred working to sitting around trying to keep himself amused.

Summers weren't so bad. When the weather was mild he could find plenty of things to do outdoors, but the weather was mild for such a short time, and then it was back to snow and being indoors; there wasn't enough to do indoors. He had built more bookshelves than he could ever possibly use; he had painted and repainted the rooms to death, and he couldn't possibly justify building even one more closet. Most of them were empty as it was.

Of course, when Maggie was in town there were still long stretches of the weekend when he didn't see her because she was doing things with friends and spending time with her family, or sometimes, and this happened more and more often, she brought home some studying to do.

Richie figured he needed an indoor hobby. It was just that he hadn't yet come up with one that held his interest. While he essentially enjoyed gardening, house plants didn't interest him. There was something about plants that grew in pots that seemed fake to him, or at least unnatural.

He didn't enjoy watching television by himself. He enjoyed stopping by a bar to watch a ball game occasionally, but it wasn't the same watching one at home, when he was the only person cheering the team on. That left reading, which was fine; he enjoyed a good mystery. But a book didn't take an entire weekend to read and the rest of the time he just sat around waiting for Monday to come so he could go back to work.

Living alone really didn't suit Richie. Some of his married friends would joke around with him and tell him he had it made, that he could do what he wanted when he wanted with no one to complain about it, but sometimes he felt that he'd rather have someone around to complain about it. On the occasions when Maggie would spend the night, he loved getting up in the morning and having someone to talk to, someone to share in fixing breakfast, someone to just be there so if he said something out loud he wasn't talking to himself.

That was why he hadn't minded at all doing a little official work on a Saturday. As soon as he had pulled into town and parked, he spotted the sheriff right away. One of her kids was with her, the boy, and when he joined them Ben said, "Nothing's happening at all, but we're going to wait anyway even though it's freezing outside. Hi, Richie."

"Good morning, Ben. Good morning, Sheriff."

Phoebe's Deputy

"I don't think they picked a good day for a rally," Phoebe said. "The only women in town are inside shopping."

Richie looked around and didn't see Billy anywhere, which was rather surprising. If anything was happening in town that he could possibly heckle, Billy was always there. Maybe a retired Billy was going to mean a changed Billy, but he doubted it.

He was about to say something like that to Phoebe, when the door to the Willy's Store opened and three women came out, carrying bags of groceries. The crazy ladies immediately went into action, standing up straighter and smiling predatory smiles.

The sheriff's sister, Mavis, spoke right up. "Women, are you tired of doing the grocery shopping each and every week for a man who no longer notices what you cook?"

The shoppers, keeping their eyes averted from Mavis, tried to pass the commune women on the sidewalk, but their way was effectively blocked.

Mavis spoke fast while she had a captive audience. "Are you tired of being a pawn in a man's world? Are you tired of doing twice the work while they're making all the money? Would you like to live somewhere where everyone is equal and the work is distributed equally?"

"I'd like to be able to walk on the public sidewalk, is what I'd like," said one of the shoppers, and the other two nodded in agreement.

"I think we're going to have to clear the sidewalk," Richie said to Phoebe, but by the time he said it the women had walked into the street and bypassed the group.

"They've got you brainwashed," Mavis called after them, and one of the men standing around yelled back, "You know what *you* need, lady?"

"They're in the wrong place," Phoebe said. "Maybe on a street corner of some city they'd get someone to listen to them, but the women here have all heard it before. And even if they were interested, it's too cold to stand around and listen."

"What's brainwashed?" Ben asked.

Before Richie could answer him, Phoebe said, "That's when you put your brain in the washing machine, honey."

And while Ben was silent, as though thinking that over, and Richie was wondering if he should offer a more precise definition, a small figure suddenly appeared from behind the men.

"Oh, dear," said Phoebe, who also saw Noggie. "I didn't think he'd really show up."

Noggie looked back at the men and then straight ahead to Mavis. "It's not brainwashing," he said, "it's all a matter of size. The big people get everything their own way, and the little people are left to suffer."

"This is *our* rally," said Mavis in a very annoyed tone of voice. "If you want to make a speech, please do it somewhere else. We were here first."

"I don't want to make a speech," Noggie explained. "I came here to hear you. But it's a truth, and you ought to learn it. If you women were bigger than the men, they'd be the ones looking for equality."

"It's not a question of size," Mavis argued. "It's a question of power. Right now, the men have all the power, and because of this, the women are oppressed."

"You don't understand," Noggie said, stepping closer to Mavis. "It's because of their size that they have the power. When have midgets ever had any power in the world? Can you name one world leader in all of history who has been a dwarf?"

"What're you, some kind of nut?"

"I'm not the nut," Noggie said. "I'm not the one who dances around every month when the moon is full. And wearing a nightgown."

"We came out here to hold a rally," Mavis said, "and you're disturbing our peace."

"This is a public place. You can't build a wall of snow here to shut me out."

"It's you!" Mavis exclaimed. "You're the weirdo who's been spying on us."

"I wasn't spying on you. I was admiring your lifestyle, that's all. I want to join your commune."

"We're a women's commune," Mavis said, stressing the word *women* heavily.

"Well, I call that discrimination," Noggie said, stressing the word *discrimination* equally as heavily. "And if I can't join your commune, then it's you who are oppressing me."

"We started that commune to get away from people like you!"

"You don't even know me. I'm as much of a feminist as you are. I have never oppressed a woman in my life!"

"That's because you're so small you probably never got a chance!"

"See? Now you're using size against me. You're just as bad as you say the men are."

Mavis looked across the street and called out, "Sheriff? I want this man arrested. He's harassing us and making it impossible to continue the rally."

The men now all turned to look across the street. Some of them waved to Richie; the rest were staring at Phoebe.

"What's this wall of snow he mentioned?" Richie asked her.

"I don't know."

"Do you think we ought to break it up?"

Phoebe grinned. "I don't know about you, but I think it's pretty entertaining. Let's see what happens."

"I think he's right," Ben said. "I always have to do what adults say because I'm smaller than they are."

"Maybe you'd like to go over there and give a speech about children's oppression," Phoebe suggested.

"I don't know what oppression means."

The women from the commune had now joined hands and formed a small circle and were beginning to sing "We Shall Overcome." Noggie, not to be outdone, ducked slightly under a pair of hands so that he was in the middle of the circle, singing even more loudly than the rest. Mavis, a disgusted look on her face, dropped the hands she was holding and walked to the curb. "Phoebe, are you going to help us or what?" she yelled across the street.

PHOEBE KNEW THAT MAVIS wasn't going to be happy until she stepped in and acted the part of sheriff. She knew it was a little display of power on Mavis's part, showing the part of the town that was watching that she had influence with the new sheriff.

"Let's cross over," she said to Richie, and grabbing hold of Ben's hand, she went across the street, where she was greeted by Noggie like a long-lost friend.

"This man is making a mockery of our rally," Mavis complained, talking to Phoebe right over Noggie's head, which reached to Phoebe's chest and Mavis's nose.

"To be honest, Mavis," Phoebe said, "he was the only one who was holding the crowd's interest. And for that matter, the crowd is all men. In fact, I'm not at all sure that rallies in downtown Greensboro Bend serve any purpose at all."

"You're as bad as Billy Benson."

"Did I harass you?"

"No, you didn't do anything except stand across the street and laugh at us."

"She's magnificent when she's angry, isn't she?" asked an enthralled Noggie.

"Just keep it up," Mavis said, "and you'll really see magnificent."

Peggy interrupted with a tentative smile. "Mavis, Patsy and I are going to do some shopping as long as we're in town. We'll see you back at the farm."

Marian and Deborah also made excuses and deserted their leader, and then Noggie said, "Why don't we all go somewhere and get a cup of coffee?"

"Good idea," Richie said, and Phoebe was about to agree, thinking that if Mavis sat down and talked to Noggie she would see just how harmless he was.

Mavis, however, sometimes preferred action to talk, and this appeared to be one of those times. With no advance warning of what she was about to do, she reached out with both arms and shoved Noggie into the street. Noggie ended up on his rear end in a pile of snow in the gutter.

"I believe that was assault and battery," Richie said, more for Phoebe's benefit than anyone else's she was sure.

But it was Mavis who said, "So lock me up if you're so smart."

Ben had gone over and helped pull Noggie to his feet. "You're right. When you're little, people are always being mean to you."

Noggie, not in the least upset by his plunge into the snow, brushed himself off and assumed a marginal karate stance. "Try that again, gorgeous."

The second time Noggie landed in the snow Ben didn't even go over to help him up. Phoebe, thinking someone had to help the poor man, said, "All right, Mavis, that'll be enough. Either clear out of here now or I will arrest you, for creating a disturbance."

"I was provoked," Mavis said. "You heard him."

"Guess what, Aunt Mavis, I have a cat," said Ben. Mavis ignored him. "I'll leave," Mavis told Phoebe, "but I want that maniac out of the cemetery. If he's not out of there by Monday, you had better post your deputy over there to guard his life."

Noggie, who had gotten to his feet a little more slowly this time, still managed one last riposte. "You can come over and guard me anytime you want, beautiful." Needless to say, he was speaking to Mavis, not Richie.

As soon as he had landed in the snow for a third time, Mavis took off down the street. When Phoebe turned around to see how Noggie was, he was still sitting in the snow, seeming hesitant to get back up. "Is she gone?" he finally asked.

"She's gone," Phoebe said.

"She is certainly a vixen, isn't she?"

That was a more complimentary term than was usually applied to her sister, Phoebe thought. "I get the feeling she doesn't like you, Noggie," she said, reaching down a hand to help him up. "But don't worry about it, she doesn't like any man."

"I thought she was glorious." Noggie was undaunted by his forays into the snow.

Relieved that it was over, Phoebe said to Ben, "Go inside and find your sister, honey, and tell her we're going."

Instead of instantly obeying, Ben turned to Richie. "You want to come over to my house and see my cat?"

Phoebe thought Richie would look amused, but instead he said, "I'd like that, Ben." That left Phoebe to wonder why Richie would want to waste part of his day seeing her son's cat.

"That is if you don't object," he said to her when Ben had gone racing into Willy's to find Dory.

"I don't object in principle," Phoebe said, "only it isn't his cat. He keeps bringing other people's cats home with him, except this time he's brought the same cat twice."

"You sure you don't mind a visitor?"

"You want to see how the boss lives, huh?" At his grin she added, "You're welcome to come over. I can fix us all some lunch. Why don't you come, too, Noggie?" she asked him, thinking he might like a break from the tent. Once Ben showed the cat around, though, she had no idea what she'd do to entertain them.

Ben returned with Dory, who was carrying three new crossword puzzle magazines. She didn't appear to be as excited as Ben at the prospect of visitors and was giving Noggie looks, as though wondering who the little man was.

Noggie and Richie followed them home, and after Ben had dragged the cat out from beneath his bed and carried him downstairs and after Richie and Noggie had duly admired him, Phoebe excused herself to put on some soup and make some grilled cheese sandwiches.

When she returned to the living room to tell them that lunch was ready, Richie was on the floor with Ben, assembling a robot he had gotten for Christmas that Phoebe had never been able to put together, and Noggie and Dory were on the couch, doing crossword puzzles in silence.

During lunch, the children found out that Noggie lived in a cemetery, and after that he was besieged by questions concerning ghosts. Noggie, with an apologetic glance at Phoebe, began telling them all the ghost stories he had heard as a child and had since forgotten.

"Ghost stories shouldn't be told over lunch," she said at one point, and when Ben protested, she added, "Ghost stories should be told in the dark at a slumber party."

"Let's turn off the lights and have a slumber party," Ben suggested.

"I tell you what," Noggie said. "Some night maybe your mother will let you spend the night in my tent in the cemetery. That's the proper place to tell ghost stories."

Ben, eyes wide, appealed to his mother. "Please, Mom, could I?"

"What about me?" asked Dory, which was so unlike her Phoebe thought she must have become instant friends with Noggie while Phoebe had been in the kitchen.

"Where do you live?" Phoebe asked Richie, hoping to change the subject, as she didn't think a night in a cemetery was quite the thing for her children.

"Nowhere as interesting as Noggie." Richie smiled. "But I do have several thousand Christmas trees on my property."

Ben's eyes had grown even wider at this news. "With ornaments and lights on them?"

Richie laughed. "No, Ben, but I cut one down every year to bring in my house."

Phoebe was sorry when lunch was over and the men made excuses to leave. She could tell they weren't really anxious to leave, and both she and the children had enjoyed their company, but since she'd be seeing both of them at the party that night she didn't try to prolong their stay. Ben tried, but when he found out he was going to see them that night at his grandmother's tavern, he didn't make a fuss.

"Are we really going to that party with you tonight?" Dory wanted to know after the men had left.

"I thought you'd like to, honey. You don't see that much of your grandma."

"We'll probably be the only kids there, Mom. Why don't you just let us stay home?"

"Because I don't want you alone at night, that's why. But if it gets boring for you, my mother has a small TV set in her office you can watch."

She didn't get any arguments after that, which made her glad, once again, she didn't allow television in their house. It was far too easy a means to bribe children with.

RICHIE SAW PHOEBE DANCING with Daryl when he entered The Greenery and he took a seat at the bar. He ordered a beer from Katie Lou. Beer was on the house since Katie Lou was throwing a party, but hard liquor was not. Richie hoped that Katie Lou didn't think he was being cheap by just drinking beer, but that was all he ever drank.

"I don't see Billy around," he said to her when she brought him a mug of draft.

"It's strange, Richie, but he hasn't been in at all since the night Phoebe drove him home."

"I expect he feels the fool after announcing his unrequited love for you in front of everyone."

"I have a feeling you're right," said Katie Lou, "and I wish now I'd been gentler with him. It just took me by surprise, that's all. He'd never even asked me out."

"I've never known him to be interested in a woman."

"I've seen him interested, Richie, but it was as though he never knew what to do about it. A little surprising, since he's a big mouth in every other respect."

"Give him a few days and I expect he'll be back. Then you'll be wishing he'd stayed away."

It had been a good day and Richie enjoyed a party now and then. Now there'd only be Sunday to get through and the weekend would be over.

Phoebe's Deputy

He spun the barstool around forty-five degrees so that he could watch the dancing and he saw that Noggie was dancing with the sheriff's daughter. His first thought was that Noggie was dancing with her because she was the only female there no taller than he was, but on second thought, Richie figured he was doing it because he wanted to. Noggie had hit it off with Dory as soon as they found out they had crossword puzzles in common.

Richie had hit it off with Noggie, too. When they had left Phoebe's house after lunch, Richie had taken him over to see his house. Noggie had duly admired all the additions and improvements Richie had made to it, but said he was enjoying living in a tent so much he didn't think he'd ever live in anything else again.

"Plus it's so easy to move around with a tent," Noggie said. "I can take it anywhere and just set up house. I'm thinking of going up to Canada this summer."

Richie wondered what he did for a living that he could just pick up and move when he wanted to and he figured it wasn't something too personal to ask, and so he asked him.

"I own a parking lot," Noggie had replied.

Richie must have looked mystified at the answer, because Noggie went on to say, "It's in Boston. I was a psychologist there, but I got tired of hearing people's problems, so I saved my money until I got enough to buy a parking lot, then I hired someone to run it. The profits after expenses are enough for me to live on if I'm frugal."

"My girlfriend's studying to be a psychologist," Richie said.

"I thought the sheriff was your girlfriend."

"No." Richie was surprised that Noggie had gotten that idea.

"I thought you were good together."

"We just work together," Richie said, wondering how Noggie could have thought they were good together when they hardly knew each other.

He shifted his gaze to where Phoebe and Daryl were dancing. Daryl was a good dancer, his hips going a mile a minute, but Phoebe's body appeared stiff. She was bouncing on the balls of her feet more than anything else, the rest of her body barely moving. Richie wasn't much of a dancer himself—at least, that's what Maggie was always telling him. Maggie loved to dance, but then Maggie was still in school. Richie didn't see why a man of thirty-four had to enjoy dancing.

He supposed he'd have to ask Phoebe to dance, since the party was for her and it might look rude if he didn't. He'd wait for a slow tune, though, if that jukebox of Katie Lou's had any slow songs.

The door to The Greenery opened and Richie watched as the crazy ladies from the commune came in. It was just three of them. The two sisters who looked enough alike to be twins weren't with them. Richie could feel the air of expectancy that filled the bar. It wasn't often that Greensboro Bend got so many single women in one place at the same time, and all the single men were looking hopeful. Or maybe not so much hopeful as challenged. That's what the single men in town considered those women, a challenge. They were all sure that the only reason a woman would want to live with other women was that she couldn't get a man.

Richie had always rather agreed with that theory, until he had met Mavis. Now he wasn't so sure. If ever there was a woman who was out to give men a hard time, that was the one.

The record came to an end and Daryl and Phoebe came over to the bar. Richie thought of asking her to dance, but she looked as though she could use some refreshment, instead, so he didn't. But when one of the troopers asked her to dance, he was sorry he hadn't.

MAVIS HADN'T WANTED to come to the party, but when her mother said, "You're the one who got her into this, the least you could do is show up at her party," Mavis had reluctantly agreed. Besides, Marian and Deborah had been looking forward to it. She had a sneaking suspicion they were there to meet men, which meant she'd have to keep a close eye on them. If any more of the members of the commune moved out, she was going to have a hard time coming up with her portion of the expenses.

Mavis saw the obnoxious trespasser dancing with her niece and walked all the way around the perimeter of the room in order to avoid coming within fifteen feet of him. When she got to the bar her mother said, "Glad you girls could make it," making Mavis bite her tongue rather than correct her mother one more time for calling them "girls" instead of "women." She knew she had to make allowances for women her mother's age.

A man who looked like a state trooper, and probably was one, asked her to dance. She told him to get lost. When he asked Deborah, Deborah politely declined when she saw that Mavis was listening. His third choice, Marian, however, gaily followed him to the dance floor. Marian was a frequent backslider.

Mavis saw that Phoebe's deputy was watching all this with a look of being entertained. He was the best-looking man in the place, Mavis concluded, if only because he wasn't trying. He had his hair cut instead of styled; his clothes were just put on rather than put together; and he didn't have the misguided notion that facial hair meant machismo. He was the type of man who would have appealed to her in her youth, the type of man who no doubt appealed to Phoebe today.

But, then, Phoebe had never been smart about men.

That ex-husband of hers was a good example. A more boring man Mavis had never met, and Mavis had met quite a few. He was the type of man who rushed out to buy a home computer when they came on the market, then set up programs on it for every phase of their life. She could remember the bulletin board that took up an entire wall in Phoebe's kitchen, filled with printouts of daily work schedules.

He was also the type of man who was into self-improvement for everyone but himself. He had Phoebe taking aerobics classes and cooking classes and having charts made up of what colors she should wear and just about anything else he heard about. And while Phoebe was running around Princeton taking every kind of class her husband thought she should take, he was no doubt meeting his student in some room somewhere and giving her personal lessons in another kind of self-improvement. Or maybe aerobics was the word for it.

And there was another thing about him, and this was something Mavis had never told Phoebe. Ted had gone after her first. He was so intent on getting in good with their father, whose teaching assistant he was, that it didn't seem to matter to him which sister he ended up with. As soon as Mavis had made it clear to him that she wasn't interested in the least, he had switched his attentions to Phoebe. And poor Phoebe, thrilled at last to have a boyfriend, fell for him.

Some part of her was tuned in to the fact that the music had now switched to a slow tune, and she saw Dory and the little fool heading in her direction. Dory was looking flushed and happy, her glasses all steamed up, but the little fool had the sense to look apprehensive. Not that Mavis was going to start anything in her mother's bar during a party for her sister, but she just hoped he wouldn't, either.

"Hi, Aunt Mavis," Dory called. "Have you met Noggie yet?"

It figured he'd also have a foolish name. "I believe we've met," she told Dory, ignoring Noggie.

"I'm one of your aunt's greatest admirers." Noggie's remark didn't appear to please Dory.

PHOEBE COULDN'T IMAGINE why Noggie had walked right up to Mavis like that. She would have thought he'd learned his lesson after being shoved in the gutter three consecutive times. When it looked as though he were going to do something even more foolhardy—ask Mavis to dance—Phoebe intervened by grabbing Noggie's hand. "How about a dance with the sheriff?"

"I was afraid you were going to ask Mavis to dance," she said to him as soon as they were on the dance floor.

"Oh, no, I'd much rather dance with your daughter," Noggie said, his voice drifting up to her.

"Good, because I'd hate to have her make another scene tonight."

"That's all show," Noggie said. "Underneath that tough exterior is a warm, lovable woman."

Phoebe looked down at him. "Are you describing my sister?"

Noggie nodded.

"Believe me, Noggie, I've known her all my life, and warm and lovable she isn't."

"That's just a front short people have to put up."

"Maybe that's true of some people, Noggie, but I don't think my sister's ever been bothered by her height."

She was the one who had always been bothered by her height, not Mavis. Mavis had never been bothered by anything. She had always been bossy and tough and opinionated, even as a child, and if Noggie had some notion that he could get through that tough exterior to an inner warmth, good luck to him.

Maybe something Noggie had said that morning was right. Perhaps small people weren't taken seriously. Phoebe knew that right now she felt as though she were dancing with a child, not a man. Dancing with almost any man would have some kind of sexual connotation to it, but there was none with Noggie. Despite the fact that his face was breathlessly close to her chest and his hand was in the vicinity of her derriere—which she understood was because of his height and not from any ulterior motives—she didn't feel anything even remotely sexual toward him and could just as easily have been dancing with her son.

The person she'd really like to dance with was Richie. It was partly because she knew him better than she knew any of the men she had danced with, but it was also because it would satisfy some of the feelings she had been having toward him since the night before when she was tempted to get into his car. But now that satisfaction would be derived in a public place where nothing untoward could come of it. In other words, it would be safe.

His car was not safe.

Phoebe remembered when she was a girl and always had a crush on some boy. It was never a realistic crush, never the kind that could possibly be reciprocated. It was a safe crush, but any crush at all satisfied some urge within her. Sometimes the crush was on a rock star or an actor, but very often it would be on a boy in one of her high school classes and she would write his name in her notebook and daydream about what would happen if he called her on the phone.

The point was, she didn't have a crush on Richie, but she was getting that same kind of satisfied feeling of being alive to something, even though that something was all in her imagination. She hadn't felt that way in a long time and she found she missed it, that sense of possibilities.

Underneath all that philosophizing she was doing, she supposed that what she was really talking about was sex. Or at least sexual attraction. It was there with Richie, and even if nothing was ever done about it, its being there highlighted every moment they were together. It made their working together more interesting, if less peaceful, than if it hadn't been there.

She wondered if it was also there for him.

She would have thought something like that would be evident; that if it was mutual she would sense it. But she knew from experience that that wasn't true. She had never sensed it in Ted when they were dating, and yet he had fallen in love with her and married her. She had thought the whole time they were dating that it was all one-sided and at any moment he would put an end to it, yet that hadn't happened.

She was so deep in thought when the record ended that Noggie almost had to shake her. "I hope all that silence wasn't on my account," he said to her.

"No," she said. "Talking about my sister just got me thinking about things, that's all."

They walked back to the bar and she decided she'd be the one to do the asking. Maybe Richie was shy about asking his boss to dance, although he didn't strike her as shy. But it wouldn't hurt her to make the first move for once, and also, for once, the idea of it didn't even bother her.

But as she was approaching him, the words already rehearsed in her mind, her mother pulled the plug on the jukebox and she saw a cake being placed on the bar. A big cake with candles on it, and written on the cake, in chocolate lettering, was CONGRATULATIONS TO OUR NEW SHERIFF.

Chapter Eight

Phoebe was surprised by how many people her mother knew.

The Greenery had been filled with people all night: some going, some coming, some staying. They all had good things to say about her mother; some had bad things to say about Billy Benson; and most of them appeared to welcome her as the new sheriff.

Other than her mother and the women at the commune, Phoebe could count on one hand the people in Greensboro Bend she had even a nodding acquaintance with. There was the woman who delivered her mail, the man at the Texaco Station and her children's teachers. Now, of course, she knew Richie and Tracy and Daryl and some of the troopers, but until she had become sheriff she hadn't known them.

Her kids knew a lot more people than she did. A good many of the people at the party were parents of children Dory knew. And Ben, because of his proclivity for bringing home stray cats, knew all their neighbors and then some.

Phoebe was sorry now that she hadn't made more of an effort to get to know people. In Princeton she had known hundreds of people, but somehow, living in a place where it snowed most of the time, she had gotten into the habit of staying indoors and being antisocial.

And, she supposed, being divorced probably had something to do with it. There was something about being divorced that made her feel like a failure, like someone no one would want to meet. Tonight, for a change, she didn't feel like a failure. She felt like someone important, and it was a heady feeling.

When the cake had been brought out she had gone into her mother's office to get Ben, but found him sound asleep in the chair. She moved him over to the couch and put her coat over him, deciding he'd rather she took a piece of the cake home for him than wake him up.

It was ten-thirty by then and she asked Dory if she wanted to leave, but Dory was helping her grandmother pass out the cake and said she wasn't tired yet at all.

"I don't know, Sheriff," Richie said to her when she sat down next to him at the bar to eat her cake. "You summer people move up here to live all year round and manage to take over the town."

Her mouth was full of cake so she could only look at him in surprise.

"Well, just look at your family. Your mom owns the busiest bar, you're the sheriff and your sister's the main rabble-rouser in town. I can't wait to see what your kids will get into when they grow up."

Phoebe smiled at him, even though she knew there was chocolate all over her teeth. "I guess it's up to us Princeton folk to bring civilization to Vermont."

"Well, we sure appreciate it, Sheriff. Even us Indians."

"Indian? You said you weren't an Indian."

"You want to hear something funny? Keep in mind now that I went along for thirty-four years without even once having anyone tell me I looked like an Indian. Then you came along and said I look like an Indian, and then your sister said the same thing, and then I asked a couple of my friends if they thought I looked like an Indian, and they said sure. When I asked them why they had never mentioned it, they said, what for? So I got to thinking about it and I called up my mother and asked her if there was any chance I had any Indian blood." He paused to take a drink of beer, leaving Phoebe in suspense.

"And?" she prompted him. "What did she say?"

"She said my dad's mother, whom I never knew because she died before I was born, was half Mohawk."

"And you never knew that?"

Richie smiled, shaking his head. "I asked her how come it took her so long to tell me, and she said it had always been embarrassing to her that I looked like an Indian, since I didn't resemble either her or my father."

"Embarrassing?"

"I guess people were like that in those days. No one wanted to be different. Hell, I would've been proud of it. In fact, I am. Now I got a new interest in life, finding out about my ancestors."

"You could change your name, pick out an Indian one," said Phoebe, remembering being disappointed when he had first told her his name.

"Go on—pick one out for me."

"How about Running Deputy?"

Richie grinned. "That's better than I'm being called now. All night long your mother's been referring to me as 'Phoebe's deputy.'"

"Oh, dear, I'm sorry about that." That was all the poor man needed.

"*You're* sorry? I feel like an appendage."

Phoebe looked around to make sure no one was overhearing what they were saying, then said to him, "That's rather like it was when I was married. I was always referred to as 'Ted's wife.' You kind of lose your own identity."

"Is that why you left him?"

Phoebe felt a blush coming on and wished she hadn't brought up the subject of her marriage. Now she'd have to tell him the truth, that she wasn't the one who left, which somehow, whenever she told someone, made her feel as though she had nothing to offer a man. If she had had something to offer, why would her husband have left her? "I didn't leave him."

"No? I thought you did."

"I don't know where you got that idea," she said, suddenly feeling a little unsure of herself.

"I don't know exactly. I think I figured since you lived in that commune for a time that you were one of those new women who wanted their independence."

Phoebe wished she could say she was one of those new women, but it was more like Ted had been a new man. "My husband left me for one of his students."

"I sure hope he didn't teach high school."

Phoebe couldn't help smiling. "No. He teaches at Princeton."

"How'd the kids take it?" he asked, and Phoebe gave him credit for zeroing in on the most important consequence of the divorce.

"Not very well. It was a surprise to all of us. What about you, Richie, have you ever been married?" She was sure he'd say no, that he was single and free. But she hadn't realized how much she had been counting on that answer.

"Not yet. I'm seeing someone. Maggie Cunningham."

Phoebe felt as though some light that had been shining between them had just been turned off. "Why isn't she with you tonight?"

"She went skiing this weekend. She's a graduate student and I don't see that much of her."

Phoebe didn't know why she was so surprised. Maybe all men liked younger women. And why shouldn't they? Why not go for someone young with no problems rather than an older woman with children? Why not go for a younger man, for that matter? Except she wasn't interested in a younger man. She had been interested in Richie until the moment he had told her he was seeing someone else. She should've been able to figure that out for herself without having to be told. He was too good not to be taken by someone.

"You know something," said Richie, "I could be wrong about this, but I think I remember you from when we were kids."

"We spent summers up here, but I never got to know any of the town kids."

"Correct me if I'm wrong, and I hope I don't embarrass the hell out of you, but weren't you the one at the lake one summer who lost her top?"

Phoebe felt the mother of all blushes coming on. It had been the most embarrassing moment of her entire life, and now it seemed that he had witnessed it.

"I guess it was you, huh?"

"I'm afraid so." Somehow, while she was swimming out to the middle of the lake, the top of her bathing suit had come undone and gotten lost along the way. She hadn't discovered it until halfway back, and when she had, she had gotten Mavis's attention and told her what the problem was. Mavis, who had thought it was hilarious, had told everyone, and Phoebe had been forced to stay crouched in the water until Mavis finally gave in and went home to get her a T-shirt to put on. Phoebe hadn't gone near the lake the rest of the summer.

"Sorry, I should've known it would embarrass you. It wasn't something that happened frequently, though, so I wouldn't let it worry you. What I really remember was what a good swimmer you were. All the other girls came to the lake to see the boys, but you swam so much I figured you were training for the Olympics."

Phoebe, who would gladly have stopped swimming if any of the boys had talked to her, didn't know what to say.

"I liked your red hair, too."

Ten minutes ago she would have been pleased by that remark, but now she just wondered what color hair Maggie had. She'd bet it wasn't red.

"You know I haven't even had a dance with you yet, Sheriff. How about it?"

"I'd love to," she said, even though all desire to dance with him had left her. She didn't in any way ever want to be the "other woman" in any relationship. Not that he probably wanted her to be, but you could never be sure about men.

The music was slow, some old Elvis Presley record from her mother's youth that she had resurrected from somewhere. He held her loosely, but even so their bodies managed to brush against each other at times in a disconcerting way.

Now that she knew about Maggie, Phoebe couldn't think of anything else. "I'd like to meet Maggie," she said to him, hoping to find out a little more about her.

"I was telling her about you and she wants to meet you, too. She thought it was pretty great we had a female sheriff."

She probably wanted to check her out, Phoebe was thinking. Well, she was pretty sure Maggie wouldn't find her any competition.

"We've got what you'd call an open relationship," Richie explained.

Oh, no. Phoebe had heard of men using that line, but she hadn't expected it of Richie. She could imagine Ted saying that to his student. And yet to be fair, an open relationship with single people was a lot different than if you were married. As far as that went, their marriage had only been open at one end.

"I figure she has boyfriends at the university, and she probably figures the same thing about me here. The thing is, though, she has the opportunities where she is. You don't get to meet many single women around here."

Phoebe could count three in her family alone.

"I told her I'd introduce her to you, but I don't know if I'll be seeing you next weekend. Unless your sister's planning another of her rallies."

"If she does, I don't think we need to protect her. Bring your friend by the house if you want."

"Thanks, I will. Speaking of your sister, I was afraid she and Noggie would get into it again tonight, but they seem to be ignoring each other."

Phoebe looked around and saw that Mavis was behind the bar, helping their mother, and Noggie and Dory were playing pinball. She just hoped that Dory realized he was an adult and didn't develop some kind of crush on him, although it wasn't easy thinking of Noggie as an adult.

It seemed as though a lot of people had been waiting for a slow song, because the dance floor was crowded. Phoebe felt herself being crushed in closer to Richie and he adjusted his arm around her. She hoped he didn't think it had been intentional on her part. She could feel his belt buckle poking into her midriff and their heads were now almost touching. It was giving her an uneasy feeling being so close to him.

RICHIE HAD A FEELING he had blown something, but until it happened he hadn't realized there was anything to blow.

It wasn't until he was explaining his open relationship to Phoebe that it had occurred to him that it might be nice to go out with her sometimes when Maggie wasn't in town. Only by then he could tell that she wasn't buying the entire open relationship thing, which wasn't hard to understand if she'd had a husband who was fooling around on her. It probably sounded like the same thing to her.

Of course, he knew it wasn't, that in actuality all he had going with Maggie was that he saw her when she came home on the occasional weekend. But still, it was the kind of thing men often lied about. And anything he said further on the subject was bound to sound suspect.

Too bad, because he liked Phoebe. He was beginning to like her before, but today he'd come to like her quite a bit. He'd liked the way she had stood up to her sister at the rally, and he'd enjoyed going over to her house and seeing how she lived. She'd been very low-key there, not making any production about fixing them lunch, and he knew Noggie had felt as at home as he had. There hadn't been any of the formality that sometimes occurred when you visited someone for the first time.

He'd enjoyed talking to her tonight and getting to know more about her, and he'd also—and he wasn't at all sure that this was something she'd appreciate—felt protective of her when he'd heard about her husband just walking out on them like that. He didn't have much use for men who walked out on their families. He had had a sudden desire to rectify things when he heard that, to go down to Princeton, or wherever the guy was, and punch him out until he agreed to go back to them.

No, he was pretty sure Phoebe wouldn't appreciate that. It made him look at her a little differently, though, knowing she wasn't the one to break up the family.

What also was making him look at her a little differently was the way her body felt pressed up against him. He knew he had no right at all to be thinking of his boss's body—although he was human, wasn't he?—but he just couldn't help it. The thing was, they fit well together.

Maybe there was something to what Noggie had said at the rally, because there was something about dancing with Maggie that made him feel he was dancing with a child. And it wasn't her age, because she was old enough, maybe it had something to do with her height.

Phoebe, though, was exactly the right height. Instead of her head being way down below his chest somewhere, it was right up against his, and he had this big urge to turn his face a few degrees so that he could kiss her.

Of course he wouldn't do any such thing. Not in a public place with half the town watching, to say nothing of her mother being there. Anyway, he knew she wouldn't like it one bit, although he wouldn't have been so sure of that if he hadn't seen her reaction when he'd mentioned Maggie and their open relationship. He shouldn't have mentioned Maggie at all, except what the hell, in a town this size she'd hear about her sooner or later.

He hadn't told her the whole truth about that incident at the lake. He'd noticed her for more than her swimming. Hell, he noticed every girl in those days. There had been something about her long, slim legs, almost pure white compared to the other kids, that, in combination with her bright carrot-colored hair, had seemed sexy as hell to him.

The other guys he had been friends with in high school had been hung up on boobs. For Richie it had always been legs, and the longer and thinner the better. The way Phoebe's pale legs had flashed in the water as she swam had turned him on and kept him turned on most of the summer.

That was maybe the stupidest thing he could have dredged up out of his memory, because now those same long, slim legs were interacting with his legs as they danced and all he could think about was how they'd feel wrapped around him, which was turning him on now. If he didn't do something about it fast, she was going to know exactly how he was feeling.

He couldn't believe it. He was acting and reacting as though he were a high school kid again. At his age!

WITHOUT ANY WARNING, Richie stopped dancing and said, "Let's get a drink, okay? It's getting pretty warm in here."

That was fine with her, as she hadn't been able to think of anything to say to him for the past minute and a half, and when you're dancing slow with someone and not talking, it starts to feel like more than dancing.

Instead of ordering another drink, though, she said, "I think I ought to get the kids home. This is pretty late for them."

"Need some help in getting them out?" Richie asked.

"I'll wake up Ben. He'll be walking in his sleep, but we'll manage okay."

"I'll carry him out for you. No problem."

It took another twenty minutes for Phoebe to thank her mom and say goodbye to everyone, and all the while Richie was standing there with Ben in his arms, not even complaining about the weight.

When she finally got the kids in the car and thanked Richie, she was surprised to see him heading over to his car. It was still pretty early for a Saturday night.

She was even more surprised when she saw his car following hers. But, then, there weren't many roads in the vicinity, and maybe it was the way to his house, too.

When she pulled up in front of her house, though, he pulled up behind her. She didn't know what he was up to, but if he was about to put his open relationship to the test, he had picked the wrong person.

She got out of the car and was opening the back door to get a sleeping Ben out, when he came up next to her. "Want me to carry him in for you?"

Saying no would be too rude, so she nodded and let him follow her up to the house. When he followed her inside, she decided she might as well get it over with and out of the way. Then they could go back to being sheriff and deputy.

He carried Ben upstairs, and as Phoebe began to get her son's clothes off, she said to Richie, "Why don't you put some water on to boil? We could have coffee if you want."

She was still in her coat when she came downstairs and Richie already had two steaming cups sitting on the coffee table in the living room. She kicked off her boots, took off her coat and opened the closet door to put it away. As usual, making room for it took an effort.

"That the only closet you have?" Richie asked.

"That was one of the drawbacks of the house," she said, wondering why the interest in closets. "I bought a wardrobe for the sleeping loft, but I haven't gotten one for my bedroom yet."

Richie, for some reason, was now next to her, peering into the closet. "It's deep."

"Yes, and all the space in front is wasted." She wondered if talking about closets was leading up to anything. If so, it was a line she'd never heard.

"What you need," Richie said, sounding quite animated, "is double rods. You could even have shelves in the back."

"I suppose I could," said Phoebe, finding talking about the closet a lot easier than trying to think of what she'd say if he got into open relationships again.

Now he had his head poked through the hanging jackets and was asking her if the closet had a light. It did, and she turned it on.

"They don't build closets like this anymore," Richie said, seemingly fascinated. Now she began to get worried that he was going to drag her into the closet. That really didn't seem like his style, though.

Having had enough talk about her closet, Phoebe went over to the couch and sat down. She took a sip of the strong coffee, lit a cigarette and leaned back into the cushions. It felt good to take off her boots and not have to be charming any longer. Not that she hadn't enjoyed the party, but she wasn't used to talking to so many people.

Richie withdrew his head from the closet and smiled at her. "I could fix it for you if you want."

"Fix what?"

"I could build in some shelves and put up another rod. It'd give you three times the space."

"I couldn't ask you to do that," Phoebe said, wishing he'd quit with the closet, drink his coffee and go home. Let him fix up Maggie's closets if he had a yen for that sort of thing.

He came over to the couch and took a seat at the other end. "I guess that sounded presumptuous of me. Maybe you like the closet the way it is."

"I could always use more closet space," Phoebe said.

"I like building things but I've done about as much with my house as it needs. Hell, I have empty closets."

Phoebe couldn't even envision a life with empty closet space. "I'm not good at that sort of thing," she said. "I can paint and even put up wallpaper, but I'm useless when it comes to even putting up curtain rods."

"I'm pretty handy," Richie said.

Phoebe began to relax. It was beginning to look as though she had misjudged him. He was obviously more interested in her closet than he was in her. She feigned a yawn and looked over at him, but he was still looking at her closet, the door of which he had left open.

"If you've got a measuring stick, I could measure it and pick up some lumber. In fact, I've got lots of lumber in my toolshed I haven't even used."

"Richie, you don't have to do that."

"I'd like to. I enjoy doing things like that."

Phoebe, who had often wished she could afford a handyman, began to take him at his word. Maybe he liked to build things the same way she liked to decorate. "What I could really use is a pantry."

Richie brightened perceptibly. "You should see mine. I could get enough canned goods in it to last out a winter if I wanted."

Phoebe eyed him speculatively as she began to envision closets, pantries, platform beds for the children with drawers under them and, the ultimate, a garage for her car. But she couldn't impose on him like that; she really couldn't. Those were the kind of things husbands were supposed to do. Not that Ted had been any handier than she was.

"I can tell you're thinking it would be an imposition on your part," he said, "but you're wrong. But if you wanted, we could make a deal."

Phoebe's eyes narrowed as she contemplated just what kind of a deal he might have in mind.

"I've made a lot of additions to my house, but I'm no good at decorating. Now I can't say I was thrilled with the way you fixed up the office, but everyone else seems to admire it. The thing is, my house looks pretty unfinished and I don't know quite what to do with it. It suits me, but—"

"But Maggie doesn't like it?"

"Maggie?" he asked, as though he had forgotten all about her. "I don't think Maggie's ever mentioned it. I don't imagine she cares one way or another. When you're a kid you don't think about stuff like that. You leave it to your parents."

Phoebe knew a good deal when she heard it. "I'd be glad to paint and wallpaper in exchange for carpentry work. If you don't mind me bringing my kids along."

"Leave Ben here. I'll teach him how to use tools."

"Teach Dory. She's the mechanical one."

He gave her a pleased smile. "Great. She's a better age to learn anyway. How about next Saturday? You want to get started then?"

"I thought Maggie was going to be in town."

"Oh, sure, but I don't usually see her during the day."

Phoebe couldn't see anything wrong with it. It was just a business arrangement, after all, nothing that Maggie should be able to object to. And it would give both her and the kids something to do on the weekends.

Richie finished his coffee and stood up. "If you have something I can measure with, I'll get that done now, and then tomorrow I can look in my toolshed and see what I need."

"All I have is a ruler."

"No, that's no good," he said. "How about if I came by tomorrow—would that bother you? I could take the measurements and then get out of your way."

"Fine," said Phoebe, "we ought to be here all day."

He was putting on his jacket and looking really pleased with himself, and she was afraid she had misjudged him. He seemed far more interested in adding to her closet space than in adding to his open relationship.

But then, just as she was starting to open the door so he could leave, she found she hadn't misjudged him at all. In an awkward move, and with his eyes closed—as though, if he didn't see what he was doing, it wasn't really happening—he grabbed her by the shoulders and pulled her to him, and then his mouth was closing over hers.

She knew she should pull away, maybe make a joke of it. She knew neither of them had any business kissing the other, not with Maggie's presence as palpable as their own labored breathing, but she didn't pull away; she stayed for the duration. There was something really wonderful about being in a man's arms again and being kissed in a very satisfactory way, and it wasn't as though she hadn't fantasized this moment, because she had thought of it off and on since she had met him and mostly on the entire time they had been dancing.

And what was a kiss between friends anyway? Well, that wasn't quite the case. She didn't know about him, but she wasn't feeling friendly; she was feeling wanted and wanted him in return, and that wasn't the sort of thing one felt about friends.

He was also a terrific kisser. She felt as though she could stand there forever, pressed securely between

Richie and the front door, and never tire of the feel of his lips getting to know hers.

They were both a little breathless when he finally pulled away and they faced each other. Richie tried to make light of it, his lips curving up about halfway into a smile as he said, "Hell, what's a good-night kiss between friends, right?"

"I couldn't agree more," Phoebe said, wishing he'd give her a second good-night kiss. Maybe a third.

"You're pretty nice to kiss, you know that?"

She could think of nothing to say to that, so this time she managed to get the door open, and this time, instead of kissing her, he gave her a pat on the shoulder.

And for a few moments, as she watched him walk to his car, she hated him and she hated Maggie and she hated open relationships in general. But she consoled herself with the thought that even though it might be nice to have a man around, closet space would be even better.

Chapter Nine

Phoebe's deputy had taken a call late on Tuesday, and when he hung up he informed his boss that the first real police business in her career was going to take place the following morning when they transported a prisoner to the state prison.

Of course, showing up at the rally might be considered police business, but since it involved her sister, Phoebe told him she didn't figure that made it quite official. Transporting a prisoner, however, sounded extremely official to her, and she was excited at the prospect.

Richie wasn't nearly as excited. Richie informed her that prisoners were usually dirtbags and she'd be better off if she never met any. But he could see that to her a prisoner was Clint Eastwood in *Escape from Alcatraz*, and he knew she was going to have to learn the hard way.

And then who should the prisoner turn out to be but Gladys Grimms, Vermont's perennial prisoner.

Phoebe took one look at the frail sixty-year-old woman wearing the same kind of granny glasses Phoebe wore, only tinted violet rather than pink, and turned her steady gaze on Richie. "Don't you dare handcuff her," her look seemed to say.

Well, Richie didn't get a charge out of handcuffing women older than his mother, but he had had prior experience with Gladys and knew she was as slippery as Route 47 in the rain. But Phoebe was the sheriff and he was only a deputy, so he deferred to her position if not to her judgment.

"Let her sit in the front beside me," Phoebe took him aside to say, and Richie was more than happy to do so. Being handcuffed to Gladys in the back seat had given him sore shins on more than one occasion. Like Phoebe, Billy Benson had also had a soft spot for Gladys, but not soft enough to let her go uncuffed.

When they got into the car and Phoebe told Gladys to buckle up, Gladys, who had been known to tell people to stuff it for less, put on her seat belt as sweet as you please. Richie immediately sensed trouble. When Gladys went into her "grandmother who does nothing worse than leave the chocolate chips out of cookies" act, watch out.

"I'm really sorry to have to do this," Phoebe said to Gladys right off, apologizing for doing her job.

"Not to worry, honey," Gladys said, putting on a brave front. "All you're doing is taking me home. I've spent most of my life in the pen."

Even from the back seat Richie could see the tears glistening in Phoebe's eyes as she looked over at her passenger. "Oh, dear, what a shame," she said.

"She doesn't end up there for doing nothing, Sheriff," Richie reminded her, but all he got was a glare in the rearview mirror for his trouble. "Tell her what you do when you're on the outside, Gladys."

"I just try to help people out, that's all," Gladys mumbled.

"Help them out of their money, she means," Richie said.

"Well, we'll try to make this ride as pleasant for you as possible," Phoebe said. "You just keep an eye out for a place you'd like to eat lunch. I guess we can buy you a nice meal before you go back to prison."

"You're a dear," Gladys murmured.

For the next hour Richie was treated to the game of one-upmanship as played by Gladys. Under Gladys's questioning, Phoebe told her about her two children. Gladys claimed to have three. Phoebe, in a distressed voice, spoke of her divorce. Gladys countered with four divorces of her own. When Phoebe related how she had been elected sheriff on a technicality, Gladys topped it by saying she was being sent away on a technicality. Richie wished he had some way of recording the conversation. He was sure he could sell it to the soaps and make a lot of money.

Lunchtime found them with nary a fast-food place within miles. With Gladys complaining that her stomach was growling, Phoebe pulled in to the parking lot of an inn that Richie knew served meals beyond his means. He didn't protest, though; his stomach was also growling by that time. And he was also getting tired of listening to Gladys, who just might shut up with her mouth full of food.

Gladys started off with escargot. "Oh, my, look at that," she said, pointing out the item on the menu to Phoebe. "That's something you'll never see on a prison menu. I'll probably live the rest of my life without ever having tried escargot." She pronounced it wrong, but no one bothered to correct her.

"Order it," Phoebe said. "It's my treat."

Well, that might not have been so bad, although the price of it would have bought them all lunch at most restaurants. She went on from there, though, alternating between whining and cajoling, until she had ordered enough items to feed an entire cell block. Phoebe, who maybe couldn't read the small print on the side of the menu that listed the prices, didn't seem upset by it, but Richie was steaming. That sneaky reprobate was conning Phoebe and he didn't like it.

Gladys ate about a third of the food she ordered, requesting that the waiter wrap up the rest to go. He looked startled enough at that request; Richie wondered how he'd look if he knew where the food was going.

They were just finishing up their coffee and mousse cake, when Gladys, with a girlish whisper to Phoebe, said she'd like to visit the facilities.

"She wants to go to the john," Richie interpreted when he saw Phoebe was at a loss. "Go with her." Phoebe seemed to get his meaning as she followed Gladys through the dining room and into the bar. Knowing Gladys's proclivity for escape, Richie kept an eye on the front door.

He really couldn't complain. Transporting Gladys, tiresome as she was, was more interesting than sitting around the office, waiting for something to happen. He could tell it was getting on Phoebe's nerves, and it was surely getting on his. He was wondering whether criminals committed criminal acts just to give the police something to do, when he saw Phoebe—alone— loping toward their table.

"Where's Gladys?" he asked, although he would rather not know.

"She's gone."

"Where'd she go?"

"I don't know. One minute she was there, and the next she wasn't. I went into the stall—"

"You what?"

He didn't wait for her to explain just why she'd left Gladys alone; after all, he could have spelled it out for her. He got up and ran out of the restaurant, ready to draw his gun if necessary, but knowing that Gladys wouldn't get far. It was open country all around the restaurant with nowhere to hide. Unless some misguided driver had given her a ride, of course.

He was halfway through the parking lot, looking into the other cars just in case, when the maître d' caught up with him.

"You neglected to pay your bill," he was informed in tones just this side of outrage.

"This is police business."

"I'm sorry, sir, but we don't subscribe to the practice of feeding law enforcement officials on the house."

Richie gave him an exasperated look. "Listen, buddy, we have an escaped criminal here. Go talk to the sheriff if you want your money, but stay out of this, okay?"

At that point Phoebe caught up with him. "Have you found her, Richie? I can't lose my first prisoner."

Squinting in the glare from the sunlight on the snow, Richie caught a glimpse of a blue blur behind a tree. Gladys's blue macintosh—he'd bet his life on it. "Stay here," he said to Phoebe, drawing his gun and starting to move, but Phoebe grabbed his arm.

"Don't you dare draw a gun on Gladys!" she cried in her mother voice again, which Richie was getting used to.

"What do you think, she's going to come back if I talk sweetly?" He pulled his arm out of her grasp and set off in the direction of the tree.

Phoebe ran after him. "Don't you dare, Richie Stuart. She's a human being, not some poor animal you hunt down and kill."

"I don't hunt," he told her.

"Well, I'm glad to hear it. Then be humane and put away your gun. You'll just frighten her with it."

"That's the point, Sheriff."

They were within a few yards of the tree. Richie called out, "Come out of there, Gladys, with your hands up."

"He's going to shoot me," Gladys screeched.

"No, he is not," Phoebe said. "I guarantee nothing's going to happen to you, Gladys. We'll all go back to the restaurant and have a nice cup of coffee."

"You never learn, do you?" Richie asked.

"Just let me handle this," Phoebe said.

Gladys peered around the tree. "I'll give myself up if you have the gun, Sheriff. I don't trust him an inch."

"Let me have your gun, Richie."

"Are you crazy? You don't even know how to use it."

She turned to him, and he would've bet she had a gleam in her eyes, only her glasses were fogged up, so he couldn't be sure. "That's the point," she said. "If you don't know how to use it, you can't hurt anyone."

That made about as much sense as not putting warnings on bottles of poison. He put the safety back on and slipped the gun in his holster. "No one's going to use a gun, Sheriff. I don't go around shooting people, despite what you might think."

"Just let me hold on to it so that she feels secure. I'll put it in my handbag if that makes you feel better."

"What would make me feel better, Sheriff, is if you'd go back in and pay the bill and let me handle this."

"How am I going to get any experience if I never get to do anything?"

"Phoebe, this isn't the time for lessons, okay?"

"Please address me as 'Sheriff.' There are times like this that I don't think you take me seriously."

"At times like this you don't deserve to be taken seriously. If you want to feel useful, go radio the state police that we have an escaped prisoner."

"I'll do no such thing. You think I want this on Gladys's record? You go start the car and I'll get Gladys. And that's an order."

Some sense of unease made Richie turn his head, and there was Gladys, at least fifty yards farther across the snow and moving fast. And behind them, in the parking lot, was an audience of interested onlookers.

Some days he thought he'd be better off being a carpenter.

As though secure in the knowledge that she had given an order and it was going to be obeyed, Phoebe marched off across the snow, her boots sinking in so deeply that she looked six inches shorter every six seconds.

Richie trailed after her. It wasn't as though Gladys were really going anywhere; all there was as far as he could see were expanses of snow-covered fields. It could be a long walk, though, long and wet. But boy, how that old lady could move.

IT SEEMED TO PHOEBE that she spent half of her life feeling stupid.

She should have known that you don't go into a rest room with a prisoner and then use the facilities behind a closed door. But Gladys had seemed properly occupied and they were out in the middle of nowhere. Besides, how was she to know the woman would betray her trust by taking off like that?

Not that Phoebe blamed her. It must be horrible to be locked up, and Gladys had no doubt panicked at the thought of it. Poor woman, it didn't seem right to lock up a woman her age. She didn't see how justice was being served by putting her behind prison bars instead of allowing her to grow old with dignity.

She certainly moved fast for someone her age. It was all Phoebe could do to keep up a decent pace, but Gladys was fairly flying across the snow.

Phoebe was a disgrace to her uniform. Richie had no doubt lost all respect for her, and the whole town would find out about how she'd let a prisoner escape if she didn't catch up with Gladys. She wasn't sorry about the gun, though. She wondered what it was about men that made them feel more in charge with a gun in their hands. All it was going to take with Gladys was a little human kindness, the knowledge that someone cared.

"You better move a little faster," Richie called, "she's gaining ground."

"I'm moving as fast as I can."

"If she makes it to those trees we're in trouble."

"That's miles away."

"It's not that far—it just looks it with all the snow."

Phoebe thought about the woman lost in the forest all night, dying from the elements. She couldn't allow that to happen.

"Maybe you ought to call the state police," she said.

"We'll get her."

"What if we don't? What if she gets lost in the woods?"

"She's criminal, Sheriff, not suicidal. Believe me, she'd rather be back in a prison cell than out in the woods. She's just enjoying making a fool of you. Of us. She's probably laughing right now."

"I don't believe that. She liked me."

"She liked not being handcuffed and she liked getting a good meal, but I don't think she's going to be writing you letters from prison. Gladys looks out for herself. She doesn't care about anyone else."

"She cares about her children," Phoebe said, remembering the way Gladys's voice had cracked when she had mentioned them.

"She doesn't have any children. She just likes spinning a story, that's all."

Phoebe tripped and fell facedown into the snow. Her legs felt leaden and she felt like staying there and never getting back up. She had eaten far too much for this kind of exercise, plus she wasn't used to trekking through the snow.

Richie reached out a hand and pulled her to her feet. "Had enough, Sheriff?"

"Whether I have or haven't is beside the point. We have to get her, Richie."

Phoebe's Deputy

"Could we try it my way?" he asked, his hand going to his gun.

Phoebe cupped her mouth with her hands and yelled out, "Gladys, please come back!"

Gladys had the audacity to turn around and wave to them.

"Look," said Richie, "if you want to fire me for this, go ahead." He took his gun out and fired it into the air. At the sound of the report, Gladys hit the ground.

"You've killed her," Phoebe moaned, her eyes wide with shock.

"I shot in the air," he said, putting an arm around her shoulders.

She shook off his arm. "Then why did she fall down?"

"Because she's smart, that's why. She didn't know for sure that I was shooting in the air."

Phoebe didn't believe him. Maybe he thought he was shooting into the air, but the wind could have caught the bullet and brought it down on Gladys. Phoebe was moving as fast as she could, stumbling through the snow, when she saw movement ahead of her. Gladys was slowly getting to her feet, her hands held up in the air.

"What did I tell you?" Richie said from behind Phoebe. "Watch this."

She turned in time to see him taking out his gun again and holding it high. Gladys's voice came immediately, shouting, "I give up, I give up."

With a chuckle, Richie put his gun away. "Guns can be very effective at times."

Phoebe wasn't about to agree with that, even if it was true. "Be nice to her," she warned him. "Let's not have the rest of the trip unpleasant because of this."

"Right, Sheriff," he said, but he sounded as though he were laughing at her.

Phoebe approached Gladys, smile in place, ready to offer the older woman comfort. She saw the answering smile as she got within feet of Gladys, then saw that it was being directed toward Richie, not her.

"Listen," Gladys said to him, "do I have to ride in the front seat with the bitch the rest of the way?"

"SHE REALLY HAD THE NERVE to say that, Mom?"

Phoebe smiled with pleasure. It was new for her to be able to have something interesting to contribute at the dinner table. Now, instead of their entire conversation focusing on what Dory and Ben had done in school that day, she got her turn to tell them about what she had done as sheriff. And today's episode had kept them enthralled.

Dinners with them had always been a pleasure, but now that pleasure was heightened in the knowledge that what she did was as interesting to them as what they did was to her. It added another element to dinners, rather like dessert.

She added the topping to the chocolate pudding by saying, "The last thing that she did before they locked her up was give me a good kick in the shins." She pulled up her pant leg to show them the bruise.

Ben could barely contain his excitement. "She did that to you? Why didn't you have her arrested?"

"She was already arrested, stupid," Dory said, but she was also smiling at the news.

"I almost forgot," Ben said. "I have a note for you."

He ran out of the kitchen and Phoebe said to Dory, "Is it from his teacher?"

"I don't know. He didn't mention it to me."

When Ben returned with the note Phoebe saw it was from the cat's owner, saying that Ben was welcome to keep the cat.

"See? It's all right," Ben said, trying not to look too pleased. "He's my cat now, isn't he?"

"Oh, honey, I don't know about having a pet. Especially now that I'm working."

"Let him keep it, Mom," Dory said. "It will teach him some responsibility."

"That's what I should be saying, Dory, not you."

"Yes," Dory said, "but you never want us to have any responsibility."

Phoebe supposed that was true. It was just that she had always felt guilty if she delegated any of the responsibility she felt was hers. She knew there were mothers who had their kids do most of the work around the house, but until she started working herself, that was all she had to do. She would have felt totally useless if she hadn't done it alone.

"All right, Ben," said Phoebe, knowing it would be impossible to say no at this point anyway. The cat was practically a part of the family already. "Has he got a name, or do we keep referring to him as 'the cat'?"

"Cats don't need names," said Ben. "Animals don't speak the English language."

"Maybe not, but we do."

THE CRAZY QUILT WOMEN'S COMMUNE was holding a council of war. The "Berlin Wall" was the topic.

On Monday morning they had awakened and found that the wall had disappeared. What's more, there wasn't any sign of anyone having done it, such as footprints in the snow. For all intents and purposes, it had simply vanished.

Monday afternoon had been spent rebuilding the wall, although it wasn't nearly as much fun the second time. On Tuesday it was again gone. Once more they rebuilt it, only this time they took turns taking watch that night from the kitchen window. Patsy had the watch from four in the morning till six, and Patsy had fallen down on her duty. She had slept through most of her watch, and when she'd woken up the wall was gone.

"First of all," Mavis said, "it's a clear case of trespassing. He has to be on our property in order to destroy the wall."

"I don't understand how he does it," Marian said. "If he had access to heat or water in his tent that would be one thing. But he doesn't have anything to melt the snow with and I can't believe he'd be out there shoveling it away all night. Plus if he were, we'd see mounds of snow in the morning."

"We're going to have to spy on him tonight," said Mavis. "We obviously can't see what he's doing from this side of the wall, so we're going to have to go into the cemetery and have a stakeout."

"We'll freeze to death out there," Deborah moaned.

"It's in a good cause."

"Do we all have to be there, or can we take shifts again?"

"We can take shifts," said Mavis. "We'll put slips of paper in a hat again and draw times."

Mavis ended up with the four-to-six slot, which was fine with her. She was sure, since those were the hours Patsy had slept through, that that was when Noggie would make his move. And when he made that move, she was going to nail him.

RICHIE WAS AT THE GREENERY. A Celtics game was on and he was watching it in a desultory way, which meant that whenever he heard cheers from the spectators he glanced at the screen, but most of his attention was focused on Katie Lou.

"I can't understand it," she was saying to Richie. "No one I've talked to has seen anything of Billy lately. It's not like him not to make public appearances. Especially in bars."

"He probably took it pretty hard," Richie said. "After twenty-five years of being sheriff and then losing the election that way, it can't be easy for him."

"How's my daughter doing?"

Richie, feeling as though he were telling tales out of school but itching to tell someone, related their problems getting Gladys to the women's prison.

Katie Lou was laughing by the time he had finished. "It sounds like you're enjoying yourselves, anyway."

"I found it enjoyable, but I can't speak for the sheriff. She was a bit miffed that her methods didn't work as well as mine."

"What happened to that little blonde you used to come in here with?"

"Maggie? She's at school. She's coming down this weekend, though."

"Things serious between you two?"

"I keep asking myself the same thing, but I never come up with the same answer. I know she dates up there, and I expect she thinks I'm doing the same. Matter of fact, I was telling Phoebe about her at your party, but as soon as I got to the 'open relationship' part, she kind of froze on me."

"Ah, Richie, that's about as good a line as saying your wife doesn't understand you."

"I know it sounds that way, but it's the truth."

"Well, you have to realize that Phoebe's already been trounced on once by a man. She's not going to walk into another bad situation."

Richie could understand that all right, but it didn't seem fair. Maggie was dating, but the one person he might like to date didn't like the fact that he was also seeing Maggie. Well, he didn't much like the fact that he seldom saw Maggie. But what was he going to do about it, sign up for college classes just to be near her? And even if he did, he had a feeling she still wouldn't go for anything exclusive. If he even mentioned exclusivity, she came out with a bunch of psychological mumbo jumbo to the effect that jealousy and possessiveness were suspect traits.

And to be perfectly honest, he wasn't jealous or possessive. He was just lonely, that's all. He wouldn't much care what she did during the week if she'd just come home on weekends so he had someone to do things with.

"I'm getting worried about him," Katie Lou was saying.

"Who's that, Katie Lou?"

"Billy, of course. What if he's sick, Richie?"

"He's got relatives in town. Anyway, if he was sick we would have heard about it. Billy's never been the type to suffer in silence."

"I wish you'd do me a favor and drop by his house. Just to put my mind at ease."

"Yeah, I could do that. I've been meaning to stop by and see him anyway. Hell, it seems a little strange not to see anything of him after spending ten years in his company. I spent more time with Billy than a lot of men spend with their wives."

Richie decided he might as well do it now. He didn't have much interest in the game, and Katie Lou was too busy to keep up much of a conversation. Anyway, the things he'd like to talk to her about he couldn't bring himself to say.

It just didn't seem right to talk to the mother of the woman he was interested in. It also didn't seem right to be interested in two women at a time, but he couldn't help it. It was all Maggie's fault, anyway.

Well, no, that wasn't really true. He'd known from the beginning how she felt about things. He was the one ready to settle down, not her. But at the time they started seeing each other it had seemed worth it. She had been a lot more fun than any of the other women he had seen on and off. How was he to know he'd want more later on?

What was odd was that he hardly thought of Maggie except when he was seeing her, but he found himself thinking of Phoebe most of the time. That could be because he was seeing a lot of her, but he wouldn't swear to it. What was mystifying him most was that he was looking forward more to fixing Phoebe's closet than he was to Maggie's coming home. But that wasn't anything personal, because Phoebe wouldn't even be there. Except he also liked the idea that Phoebe would be over at his house making a few changes.

"Nothing drastic," he had told her, not wanting to end up with some feminine-looking abode. But she had told him not to worry, that she'd check with him before she made any changes.

His house could use a little fixing up. He had built all kinds of additions and improvements to it, but nothing was finished. Everything was unfinished wood, even the floors in the bathrooms.

Oh, hell, maybe he was just getting old. It sure didn't say much for his virility when he got more excited over putting up shelves than spending the night with Maggie.

When Richie left The Greenery the night was cold and clear, and he spent a few minutes heating up his car. He was wondering whether he should take a bottle with him when he visited Billy. They could have a few drinks and do a little talking. Except taking a bottle with him wouldn't be the smartest thing in the world, because very often when Billy drank he got belligerent, and he hated Billy when he got like that. Anyway, he'd feel as though he had to keep up with him, and he didn't want a hangover in the morning.

When he got to Billy's house he didn't see any lights on inside. That was okay, because it was almost midnight and Billy might already be in bed. It was a relief, actually, because knowing how much Billy loved to talk, he might have been there until the wee hours, listening to him.

He got a pencil and tablet out of his glove compartment and wrote Billy a note. He just said that he had stopped by, hoped Billy was doing okay and invited him to drop by the office.

He thought of changing that last line when he remembered what Phoebe had done to the office. He was pretty sure Billy wasn't going to be thrilled by the improvements, any more than he was. Still, the place had been home to Billy for twenty-five years and he didn't want him feeling as though he couldn't even drop by now.

He got out of the car and walked up to the door. He opened the mailbox attached outside to slip the note in, and was surprised to find it full of mail. That didn't make sense unless Billy had gone out of town, and in all the time he'd known Billy he had never known him to go out of town unless it was on police business.

He decided to walk around to the garage and see if Billy's truck was there. There was a padlock on the garage door and no window to look into, but judging by the snow piled up in front of the door, Billy hadn't gone out or in for quite some time.

Richie wasn't sure what to do. This was a situation in which people usually called the police, but he was the police. And he knew that Billy wouldn't appreciate his breaking into his house on the pretext of being worried about him.

But he really was worried. For all he knew, Billy could be in there with a broken leg or worse. Under ordinary circumstances he would call the sheriff for advice. Only all he'd be doing would be waking up Phoebe, and she'd probably just tell him to do what he thought best.

He figured his choices were either breaking down a door or breaking one of the windows. He knew if it were his house he'd prefer the door broken rather than having to replace glass.

He took a look at the front door, but it was solid. The back one, though, wasn't solid at all. In fact, it was so flimsy Richie would've replaced it immediately if it were his house. Just a slight kick opened it, and then he was in the kitchen and turning on the light.

It was a mess, but that could mean anything. Turning on lights as he went, Richie walked through all five rooms of the house, even looking into the closets. There was no sign of Billy anywhere. And judging by the lack of cigar smoke in the air, he hadn't been there in a while.

Richie felt relieved. For a few moments there he was afraid he'd come across Billy dead of a heart attack. On the other hand, he had broken into Billy's house for no other reason than that Katie Lou hadn't seen him lately.

Well, if he was lucky, Billy would never know about it. He'd just shut off the lights and lock the back door on his way out.

He'd also, just to be sure, call one of Billy's brothers the next day and find out just where he was. And if they didn't know, then it was their worry, not his.

Hell, for all he knew, Billy might be down in Florida, sunning himself on some beach. That didn't sound half bad with the temperature down around zero degrees.

WHEN THE ALARM WENT OFF at 3:45 in the morning, Mavis was sorry she had suggested the graveyard stakeout. She dressed warmly, then made herself a thermos of coffee to keep her awake and alert.

She drove to the cemetery and parked the car at the entrance. She had brought a flashlight along, but the moon was bright and she found she didn't need it.

She crept quietly through the snow, saying in a loud whisper, "Peggy, where are you?" She was almost to the tent, when she found Peggy huddling behind a ghost-shaped form that was no doubt a gravestone.

"Seen anything?" she asked her.

"No," Peggy said. "The tent's been dark the whole time I've been here and the wall's still up."

"Go on, then, I'll take over," Mavis said. She saw a smaller form and began brushing the snow off it, and when it was clear she had a two-foot high gravestone to sit on. It was as cold as ice, but at least she wouldn't soak the seat of her pants through as Peggy had done.

After a half-hour she began to think she was freezing to death. This was because, despite the coffee, she was being lulled to sleep, and she had heard this happened to people who did freeze to death. Or maybe it was people who almost froze to death. She didn't know how anyone could possibly know what happened to people who actually died of exposure.

She was just deciding to get off the stone and walk around a little to get her circulation going, when she saw the tent light up. She froze on the spot.

After that she was treated to something of a light show. There was a sudden flare of light in the tent, almost as though there had been an explosion, except that this took place in silence, and the next thing was she heard the sound of a zipper being unzipped. It was a strange sound and she wasn't trusting her hearing, until she realized it was the tent flap being undone.

She ducked behind one of the white forms, only her head peering out the side.

There was the culprit heading toward the fence, against which, on the other side, was their wall of snow.

She decided to give him a few minutes so that she could catch him in the act. Although now that she was about to, she didn't know exactly what she'd do when she caught him. Maybe it would be enough just to put a scare into him. And someone coming at him out of the graveyard might just do that.

She counted slowly to five hundred before making her move. Then, as silent as an Indian—or least she supposed she was that silent—she crept around the tent to see what he was up to.

He was ingenious; she'd give him that. He had climbed halfway up the chain-link fence and was resting his arms on the top. And extended from his arms was a pole over which a black kettle was hooked. And in that black kettle, if she wasn't mistaken, was a charcoal fire.

The little sneak! He was melting their wall at night without leaving any evidence at all. What she ought to do was roast him over his own fire.

She got within a foot of the fence and shouted, "I'm making a citizen's arrest, you rotten little sneak!"

In almost slow motion, the stick was dropped, the pot fell onto the snow wall and Noggie fell at her feet. She had the satisfaction of seeing his eyes almost pop out at the sight of her.

"How dare you!" she exclaimed. "Hanging a pot over our side of the fence is every bit as much trespassing as entering our property with your person. Get up this minute. I'm turning you in to the state police."

At least it wasn't Phoebe she'd have to contend with. Phoebe was so good-hearted she'd be inviting him in to warm up.

"You look like a goddess in the moonlight," he said to her, his voice sounding awed.

"I'll 'goddess' you! Get up off the ground and act like a man."

She thought he was obeying her, thought he was getting to his feet, but instead he reached out, grabbed her leg and pulled her down on top of him.

"One kiss before I'm locked away for life," he said to her. The next thing she knew his warm lips—no doubt from his fire—were pressed against her cold ones. And she was held in a clamp that belied his small stature.

"You're assaulting me," she tried to say against his mouth, but it came out sounding garbled.

This was the warmest she had been in ages, and like the way she had felt earlier, she had the feeling it would be more pleasurable to succumb than to fight. But she wasn't a feminist for nothing, and fight she did.

No sooner did she lift a hand to smack him, though, than he grabbed it, then grabbed the other, and she found her wrists pinned above their heads. When she brought up her knee to put it into action, his legs went around hers and pinned them.

She pulled back her head and glared down at him. "You'll pay for this, you pervert!"

"Gladly, my darling," he answered, then rolled her over into the snow.

Chapter Ten

Phoebe was at Richie's house. She was alone, since Ben, whom she thought would want to come with her, especially if there was the chance of watching television, had wanted to stay at home and watch Richie work. Dory had stayed home to help Richie and to learn basic carpentry.

He had brought Phoebe by his house the night before to get her ideas on what to do with his place. She was enchanted with all the space but dismayed by all the work to be done. The whole place was unfinished wood, the kind where you got splinters just by standing near it.

She had decided to start with the kitchen. With his okay, she was painting the ceiling and walls white, leaving the cupboards natural but oiling the wood, and putting down floor tiles that resembled red bricks. She started to mention curtains, but Richie said he didn't like curtains, that he liked being able to look out at his trees. She would have felt uncomfortable with windows anyone could just look into, but since it was his house, she dropped the idea of curtains.

He had arrived at her house that morning, given her the keys to his, and she had stopped off at Willy's and bought the paint. What was nice was she wouldn't have to worry about splattering the floor with paint, since it was going to be covered anyway.

She had bought a roller with a long handle, so she didn't have to stand on a ladder to do the ceiling. She had gotten a coat of primer and one of paint on the ceiling and the walls, and decided to take a break before putting on the second coat.

Phoebe knew it was none of her business, she knew she wouldn't like Richie doing it at her house, but she couldn't stop herself. She started to snoop around. At first she told herself that what she was doing was looking around again to see what had to be decorated. But that didn't wash. Looking into medicine cabinets and closets and drawers had nothing to do with decorating, and she planned on looking into all of them.

She went into his bedroom first. It was extremely neat, neater than hers ever looked, and she wondered if that was normal for him or whether he had cleaned up because she was coming over. Or maybe he had cleaned up because Maggie was coming to town.

There wasn't a bedspread but the bed was made. It was a king-size, larger than any bed she'd ever had. When she'd been married they had had a queen-size, and now she slept in a double.

The dresser drawers were also neat. She noted that he wore briefs rather than boxer shorts, as Ted had worn, and that among all his white underwear there was one pair in blue. She wondered where that one different pair came from, but that kind of thinking wasn't productive, as she'd never likely find out.

His closet was also neat, with uniform shirts and pants on one side, jeans and flannel shirts on the other. Shoes were evenly lined up on the bottom. The two shelves, which she would have had crammed with things, were empty.

The bathroom was clean and orderly and the medicine cabinet was disappointing. All she could tell about him from the shelves was that he shaved, and she knew that already. There was also toothpaste, looking lonely on a shelf by itself, and after that, nothing. As far as she could determine he never got a headache, a cold, bloodshot eyes or chapped lips.

In the living room, she avoided his desk. Whatever was in there was definitely too personal to snoop into, but she did take a close look at his bookshelves. There were two rows of paperbacks, all mysteries, which made sense for a deputy. There were also a couple of library books, checked out that week, on the subject of American Indians. She saw, higher up, a book that looked like a high school yearbook, and she was just lifting it down, when the doorbell rang.

Blushing with guilt, she dropped the book, then quickly reached down to pick it up and return it to its shelf. It must be Richie, finished for the day and about to catch her snooping. Thank heavens she had his keys and he hadn't just walked in on her.

Only it wasn't Richie. It was a cute blonde about the size of Mavis, dressed in jeans and a red parka. She was so relieved it wasn't Richie that she beamed at the young woman.

"Hi," she said to Phoebe, "is Richie around?"

"No, he's not. Are you Maggie?"

The young woman nodded. "You must be the new sheriff, Richie told me about you."

"I'm Phoebe. I'm painting his kitchen, if you'd like to come in."

Phoebe's Deputy

Maggie looked intrigued by the news, but didn't say anything. "If you know where he is, maybe I could use his phone to call him."

"He's at my place," Phoebe told her, "but I don't have a phone. I could tell you how to get there, though. It's not far from here."

"I'll come in for a minute, if you don't mind. I wanted to meet the first woman sheriff of Greensboro Bend anyway."

"Good. Come talk to me while I work," said Phoebe, leading the way to the kitchen. She was glad now she had stopped being overtly interested in Richie when she had heard about his open relationship. If she hadn't, she knew she'd be feeling guilty now.

Although now that she had gotten a look at Maggie, Phoebe was reasonably certain she wouldn't appeal to him. Anyone who went for cute, athletic-looking blondes wouldn't also go for tall, sedentary redheads.

THE CLOSET WAS GOING to be a model of efficiency when he got through with it. Floor-to-ceiling shelves for storage would line the back. When he had cleared out the closet he had counted only two long coats and the rest were jackets, so he was going to divide the front in two, one side with one pole and the other with two for the jackets. He had also bought a hook to put up on the back of the closet door. Sometimes you just didn't feel like hanging up your jacket.

Dory was the best helper he'd ever had. Without saying anything or even asking questions, she had listened to all his instructions and followed them exactly, and by the time he got to the third shelf, she was able to do it all by herself.

Ben didn't help at all, but, sitting cross-legged on the floor with the cat on his lap, he asked a stream of questions. Richie learned through trial and error that what Ben required was not answers to his questions so much as someone paying attention while he asked them. Dory, on the other hand, appeared to need drawing out, but in case it was more a matter of privacy than shyness, he left her alone.

When Richie heard the name Daddy spoken, though, he halted Ben in his discourse long enough to ask, "Do you see your father?"

"He doesn't live with us anymore," Ben said.

"I know that, but don't you ever see him? Doesn't he visit?"

Ben exchanged a secretive glance with Dory, who shook her head at him.

Richie was now intrigued by the secret. "Does he still live in New Jersey?"

"He lives in Princeton," Ben said. "But he's going to—"

"Shut up, Ben," said Dory.

"You just said not to tell Mom," Ben said.

"It's none of my business, Ben," Richie told him, not wanting to see trouble between the two.

Dory stared at him, as though assessing his trustworthiness. Then she said, "Can you keep a secret?"

Richie wasn't sure he ought to hear it if it was a secret from their mother, but curiosity got the better of him. "Sure."

"You absolutely promise you won't tell our mother?"

Crossing his heart, Richie nodded solemnly.

"He's coming to see us next weekend," Dory said, "only Mom doesn't know."

"I won't tell her," Richie said, "but don't you think she ought to know? That's probably not the kind of thing she'd like to be surprised with."

"She'd just cry," Ben said. "We don't like to see her cry."

"Well, it might be better if she cries when you tell her rather than when he shows up unexpectedly."

Dory shook her head. "No, she won't cry in front of him. She'll put on an act and pretend everything's fine. She always does that."

Richie thought they were wrong, that Phoebe would want to know her ex-husband was going to show up, but he didn't feel he should betray the children's trust. And maybe he wasn't right; they knew her a lot better than he did.

About all he could do, he supposed, was keep her so busy on his house next weekend that she wouldn't have time to sit around and cry. And to cheer her up, he'd get her pantry built.

"THAT SOUNDS LIKE a good trade-off to me," Maggie said, looking at the newly painted walls. "And Richie's really good at building things."

"I'd offer you some coffee," Phoebe said, "but I don't know where anything is."

"Let me." Maggie quickly found what she needed, which made Phoebe feel presumptuous for having sounded like the host, when it was Maggie's boyfriend's house, not hers.

"When do you finish school?" Phoebe asked her.

"I get my master's in June."

"I imagine Richie will be glad to have you around all the time. I'm sure he misses you when you're away at school."

"Mmm," Maggie said, which could have meant anything. Then she sighed, looking over at Phoebe. "My department head is leaning on me to go for my doctorate. I haven't made up my mind yet, but I might be staying on for another year. With my doctorate I'd have a lot more options."

Being the daughter and the ex-wife of academics, Phoebe knew what she was talking about. Then she thought of Mavis with her doctorate, tutoring high school kids, and told Maggie about her.

"That won't be me," Maggie said. "I'm pretty ambitious. I'd appreciate it if you didn't mention it to Richie, though, until I make up my mind."

"Poor Richie," Phoebe said, knowing how she'd feel in his place. Another year of a long-distance love affair would be hard to take. At least, she'd find it hard, and she figured Richie was normal in that respect.

"Oh, don't feel sorry for Richie," Maggie retorted. "We date, but it's nothing serious. There's a guy at school I see a lot more of."

"He told me you had an open relationship, but I didn't believe him." Phoebe wished now she had. She wished she had jumped at the chance of being part of that open relationship.

"I wouldn't even call it that. In fact, I figured he'd be dating you by now."

"I don't have time to date," Phoebe told her. "I have two children." And then she changed the subject, asking Maggie about the University of Vermont but not paying much attention to what she was being told, because she was thinking it would be all right to go out with Richie now if he asked her, and she only hoped he would.

It was all right, at least, as far as Maggie not caring, but not really totally all right. It wouldn't be totally all right unless Richie stopped seeing Maggie completely. Maybe it was old-fashioned of her, or even greedy, but she didn't like the idea of sharing a man.

It was something she'd have to think about.

MAVIS WAS IN BED with the worst cold she had ever had in her entire life.

The other members of the commune were solicitous, interrupting her rest every few minutes with cups of tea and bouquets of fresh flowers and offers to change her sheets. She snapped at them, one and all, just wanting to be left alone.

The wall was still up, which was a major coup for her. She had told the others she had caught Noggie red-handed and put such a scare in him that he wouldn't be melting down their wall again.

That wasn't quite the truth. In fact, it wasn't even marginally the truth. The truth was, after rolling around in the snow with him for the better part of an hour, alternately hating herself for what she was doing and loving the feel of his lips on her own, he had been the one who had finally put an end to it, getting to his feet and saying, "Come by and see me sometime."

That was all; just come by and see him. And before she could think of anything to say in reply, he had gone inside his tent and zipped it up.

Mavis had stumbled home through the snow, gotten into bed and awakened eight hours later with near pneumonia and four commune members waiting outside her door for a report.

She felt like a fool. Worse than a fool, she felt like a traitor. She was a traitor. Even now, probably on her death bed, she was devising means in her mind to see him again. Not to roll around in the snow again with him, certainly not for that. That was absolutely the last thing she wanted to do.

What she had in mind was an intellectual discussion. It had occurred to her that maybe she had misjudged him. It was always possible that there was a man out there who was really a feminist. Noggie might just be that man. And if he was, was it really fair of her to exclude him from their group?

She wouldn't mention it to the others, of course, until she found out for sure. She didn't want to get their hopes up for nothing. And if he wasn't, they needed protection from him.

She'd like to go over there right this minute and straighten it out with him. Except she was too sick to get up.

AFTER MAGGIE HAD LEFT, Phoebe didn't feel inclined to put on the second coat. Instead she cleaned the roller and the brushes she had used and drove back home.

Richie's car was still parked in front of her house, and when she got inside she found him in the living room, playing cards with the kids.

"Wait till you see the closet," Ben yelled out, but she couldn't help seeing it. It was right there with the door wide open and all the coats still piled on the floor. It was also gorgeous, just about the best closet she had ever seen.

"I didn't know where you wanted anything put," Richie explained.

"That's all right. Don't worry about it. It's wonderful, really wonderful."

He was looking justifiably pleased. "Glad you like it. How's my kitchen looking?"

"I only got the first coat on and then Maggie came by. She said to tell you to give her a call."

"Maggie? You met Maggie?"

"Yes, she came by to see you."

"Who's Maggie?" Ben asked.

"That's Richie's girlfriend," she told him, and saw her children exchanging dismayed looks. She was afraid that maybe they had gotten the idea Richie could be her boyfriend. If so, it was just as well they heard about Maggie now.

She took off her jacket and hung it in the new closet, then sat down on the floor beside them. "What're you playing?"

"He taught us hearts," Dory said, "only Ben keeps getting the queen and won't pass it to anyone."

"I'm afraid to."

"He plays hearts the way I do," Phoebe said, not liking surprises any more than Ben. At least if you kept the queen you knew where it was at all times.

"You guys eaten?" Phoebe asked.

They all shook their heads.

"Want me to fix something?"

There were nods all around.

"Okay, but I get to play with you after we eat."

It had been years since she'd played a good game of hearts. Ted and the other faculty couples had all preferred bridge. And most of the time she had ended up the dummy.

KATIE LOU WAS AT THE END of the bar, talking to Frank, when Billy's cousin, Booter, came in. Booter, like Billy, was a heavy drinker and apt to get into a fight once he was in his cups, and Katie Lou generally wasn't glad to see him walk into The Greenery. Tonight, however, she wanted to talk to him.

"Come on over here, Booter," she said, "and let me buy you a drink."

Frank looked surprised. Booter looked even more surprised. She had a feeling he knew he wasn't one of her favorite customers. Nonetheless, he took the empty seat beside Frank and said, "How's it going, Katie Lou?"

"You know how it is, Booter. Business is always great except during the mud season." Although even then some serious drinkers risked getting their cars stuck in order to satisfy their thirst.

Frank was looking a little miffed not to have her undivided attention anymore, so Katie Lou got right to the point. "I hear Billy's taken a little vacation," she said. At least, that was what Richie had said Billy's mother had told him.

"Deserves it," Booter said. "He hasn't had a vacation in twenty-five years."

"Do you know where he went?" Katie Lou asked.

Booter ignored the question until Katie Lou had brought him his free drink, which he quickly downed before answering. "I hear he headed south."

"I don't blame him," Katie Lou said. "At this time of the year I'd gladly trade this place for a beach."

"More likely he's fishing," Booter said, and Katie Lou decided he didn't know any more than she did. Anyway, Billy's whereabouts weren't important. She really just wanted to make sure he was all right. Somehow, his trip coming right after that night he'd broken up her bar made her feel somehow responsible for him leaving.

When Booter ordered a second drink and carried it over to the pinball machine, Katie Lou took some quarters out of the cash register and was about to head over to the jukebox and play some vintage Beatles, which she was feeling nostalgic for, when Frank said, "What's with you and Billy? Since when do you care where he is?"

"It's just not like him to disappear," Katie Lou said.

"You have a thing for Billy or what?"

"Frank, you know very well I don't have a 'thing' for Billy. I was just a little worried, that's all."

"I'll bet if I took a vacation you wouldn't worry about me."

"What is this, Frank, you jealous of Billy?"

"Do I have reason to be?"

Young men could be a real problem at times, Katie Lou was thinking. She decided to just ignore him and go play the jukebox. But he must have been looking for an argument, because as soon as she got back to the bar, he said, "Why do you have to play all those old songs?"

"Probably trying to recapture my youth," she told him, half kidding.

Frank, who hated any reference to their age difference, went into an immediate sulk. That was another thing about young men: they tended to sulk.

When he realized that his sulking was being ignored, he baited her with, "I think he got to you that night with his declaration of love."

"You think wrong, Frank."

"You want to know why I think so, Katie Lou?"

She didn't, but she knew she was going to hear it anyway. "Can't we just drop the subject?"

"You called him a 'fat, sloppy drunk,' that's why. Now that's not something a bartender says to a customer. That's something a woman says to a man. If she's interested in him."

"I said it to him, Frank, because he had just busted my window. What was I supposed to do, congratulate him? I lost my temper, all right?"

"You never lose your temper with me."

"I'm about to, Frank."

"All it tells me, Katie Lou, is that a fat drunk is preferable to me because he's closer to your age."

"Whom have I been seeing, Frank, Billy Benson or you?"

"I don't think it's working out, Katie Lou. You don't take me seriously."

"Not when you act like a child."

"I'm getting pretty tired of your always pointing out our age difference, too."

Katie Lou leaned her elbows on the bar and rested her chin on her hands. "Now listen to me carefully, Frank. I'm right around your mother's age. And if I occasionally refer to our age difference, it's not because it particularly bothers me, but because you're always trying to get serious. It's just a way of warning you off, that's all."

"What's the matter with getting serious?" Frank was heard to mumble into his glass.

"I was serious for thirty years," she told him. "For the next thirty years I plan on having a good time."

"With Billy?"

Katie Lou gave it up and moved down to the other end of the bar. Richie had just come in with that young woman he dated, and she thought they'd make better company. Plus, of course, they'd need a drink.

And Frank was beginning to get tiresome. Why couldn't he just find himself a woman his own age and settle down?

RICHIE WAS AFRAID Maggie had come down a weekend too late. Last week he had been dying to see her; this week he'd felt more like staying over at Phoebe's house and continuing their game of cards than he had felt like going out on a date.

Hell, he'd been dating since he was fourteen, which meant a good twenty years. He was getting a little tired of dating.

Maybe Maggie would be willing to make it an early evening. She might be getting tired of dating, too, particularly since she was obviously doing more of it.

Katie Lou came down and asked them what they'd like to drink, and Maggie said, "Hey, I met your daughter today."

"My daughter the sheriff?" Katie Lou asked, and Maggie nodded.

"I liked her."

"Phoebe's easy to like," Katie Lou said, and Richie figured she was comparing her to her other daughter.

Richie, who really didn't feel like drinking, ordered a tomato juice, but was surprised when Maggie followed suit. "If you don't feel like drinking," he said to her, "what are we doing here?"

"I just felt like talking."

"We could've done that at my house."

Maggie leaned over so that their shoulders were touching and gave him a wicked smile. "Well, the thing about talking at your house, Richie, is that one thing leads to another, and I was really hoping to make an early night of it. I'm heading back for school in the morning because I have an exam on Monday I need to study for."

That meant Maggie wasn't going to spend the night with him. Ordinarily that would have gotten a big argument out of him, but for some reason he didn't really mind. He wondered whether that was a sign of getting older or a sign of losing interest in Maggie. "That's okay, Maggie, I'm pretty beat anyway."

She smiled at him with a look of disbelief. "Your new boss is really keeping you busy, isn't she?"

"I just haven't used my muscles for a while."

"So how's it going, working for a woman?"

He shrugged. "It's a little different from working with Billy."

"I would imagine so. Do you mind taking orders from her?"

"She's not all that bossy, and when she tries to be it's mostly funny." What was really funny was that he had been dying to talk to someone about Phoebe, and then it turned out the only one who wanted to talk about her was his girlfriend.

"How is it funny?"

He told her about transporting Gladys to prison, ending up with the fact that Phoebe didn't like guns.

"I don't like them, either," Maggie said.

"Yes, but you're not going into police work."

Maggie was looking away from him, and Richie would have sworn by the expression on her face that she wanted to say something to him, but then she kind of shook her head and just sat there, drinking her tomato juice.

"Something on your mind, Maggie?"

"Lots of things, Richie, and number one is my exam coming up. But I don't want to talk about school on my one night away from there. Tell me the town gossip. That's always good for a laugh."

And so Richie amused her with stories of Noggie and Mavis and Billy busting up The Greenery, and while he was telling her he realized something was missing between them. For the first time, she was feeling more like a friend than a girlfriend. He didn't feel like touching her, other than in an affectionate way, and he got the feeling it was the same for her.

He thought it was a question of too little dragging on for too long. And that had mostly been inertia on his part. He could have ended it earlier and found himself another woman, only it had seemed easier just to go along with their arrangement.

Even though he had a feeling it wouldn't bother her one way or another if he ended it here and now, he didn't want to do it. He wanted her to be the one to break it off. That had always been one of his problems with women. He hated to do the actual breaking up, so he always stayed in relationships until well after they had disintegrated. He'd always had this idea that a gentleman let the lady do the breaking up, even if it didn't make much sense.

He also didn't want to be precipitous. Maybe he was just tired tonight. Maybe by the next time he saw Maggie he'd feel differently. And maybe Phoebe had no personal interest in him at all, which would mean he'd be ending it for no reason.

He didn't feel in any great hurry about any of it. He'd just let things take their natural course.

"IF WE WOKE UP MOM maybe she'd play hearts with us again," Ben said, eating the cereal Dory had fixed him. The regular cereal, not the kind with raisins that he liked the best. The cat had knocked that box off the top of the refrigerator and spilled it all over the floor, and Dory had made him throw it out, even though it still looked okay.

"Let her sleep, Ben. This is the only day this week she hasn't had to get up early."

"You know what Richie said, Dory? He said he could build me a tree house."

"I heard him. But we don't have a tree the right size for one, Ben."

"I wouldn't care if it wasn't in a tree."

"Then it wouldn't be a tree house."

It would be a little Ben kind of house that he wouldn't have to share with Dory. He liked sharing a room with Dory at night because he didn't like sleeping all alone, but it would be good to have a place where he could play and no one would care if he didn't put his toys away. "He likes me," Ben said.

Dory gave him the kind of look she always gave him when she knew more about something than he did. "Don't get any ideas, Ben, because he has a girlfriend. You heard Mom say that."

"You said Daddy was never coming back."

"He's married again. You know that."

"I'd like Richie to live with us."

"I know that, but it's not something kids have any say in. If we did, Dad would still be here. Adults can do whatever they want and it doesn't matter what we want."

"You like him, Dory?"

"Just finish your cereal, Ben, and I'll play some cards with you."

They were on the floor in the living room, playing hearts, when Ben heard the car drive up in front of their house. He ran to the window and looked out. "Dory, it's him. It's Richie."

"Is he coming in?"

"He is. He's coming to see us. I'm going to wake up Mom."

"I guess you better," Dory said, getting up and going to the door.

Ben sat down on the bed next to his mother and began to bounce up and down.

His mom opened her eyes, gave him a sleepy smile and said, "What time is it, honey?"

"I don't know, but Richie's here."

His mom frowned. "Isn't this Sunday?"

"Yes, but he's here. I'm telling the truth—I really am. I promise."

"Well go talk to him while I get dressed, okay?"

He had said hardly anything to Richie, though, when his Mom came out, which was the fastest he'd ever seen her dress. She was looking pleased and trying not to smile.

"What are you doing here on a Sunday?" she said to him, and then they were both smiling at each other.

"I figured I could get started on that pantry."

"What about Maggie?" asked his mom, and Ben remembered that Maggie was his girlfriend's name.

"She said something about going back to school today when I saw her last night."

And then his mom was really grinning and asking Richie if he had had breakfast, and Richie said no, he'd come over as soon as he'd woken up. Dory was looking surprised, as though maybe she didn't know everything. Ben was thinking that after Richie got finished with the pantry maybe they could all play hearts again.

It was going to be a good Sunday.

Chapter Eleven

The criminal elements appeared to be hibernating.

Richie assured her that come spring they'd have more work to do, and when summer arrived, and the summer people, they'd be kept busy all of the time. But for now, he told her, she should just enjoy the lull.

Phoebe *was* enjoying the lull, because she and Richie were spending most of their time drawing up home improvement plans. There was something about the way she was thinking about those home improvement plans, though, that was bothering her. In particular, it was the way in which she was viewing Richie's house.

She'd think about the four bedrooms he had, each with its own closet, and she would picture Dory in one of the bedrooms and Ben in another and a third could be a den or a study or a playroom or even a nursery. The last one, of course, would be hers and Richie's. Dangerous thinking, extremely dangerous, but she couldn't seem to stop.

She'd remember his couch, a nice tweed, and think about how it wouldn't show cat hair or scuff marks or food stains, and how a large family could all sit on it, curled up beside one another. The fact that an equally large television set was facing it didn't even bother her. It wasn't as though they couldn't turn the set off.

The kitchen had a couple of stools in front of a breakfast bar, but there was also room for her round table that would seat any number of people, and there was even a dishwasher that looked as though it had never been used. She and Dory and Ben could get some use out of it; none of them much liked washing dishes.

Equally as inspiring as the house was the property. It held a lifetime of Christmas trees, a stream just made for children to wade in, trees to climb and to hang swings from, and all kinds of wildlife living in the woods. She would have loved to grow up in a setting like that. It wouldn't be bad growing old in, either.

She didn't even know why she was letting him make plans to improve her house. It had never seemed like home to her, more like an in-between house. It was her own, and she liked it all right, but she had never anticipated putting the work and the love into it that she had put in the house she had had in Princeton when she was married. Actually, she had thought she'd lost her enthusiasm for fixing up places, until she started work on Richie's place. Then she realized she still had the enthusiasm, just not for a house she hadn't been happy in. Her house had always been a divorced house to her, a make-do place because she had been deprived of the real one.

Now she was thinking that a real one would be one with Richie, which was really premature thinking, as she'd never even gone out with him. And yet she wondered if dating was the criterion with adults. She had spent more hours with Richie when they were working than she'd ever spent with Ted when they were dating. And in a way this was like dating. They talked; they got to know each other; they went through experiences together; they learned how the other one thought; and he was even getting to know her children. All that was lacking was the sexual part. But despite that, she thought she knew Richie better already than she had known Ted when she'd married him.

The only thing wrong with her theory was that the relationship was no doubt one-sided. Richie certainly wouldn't be wasting his time making plans to fix up her house for her if he had any intention of ever moving them into his. And she had to wonder if she was the kind of person who was self-deluding. She had never even had a clue her marriage was in trouble; she could just as easily not have a clue what was in Richie's mind. Maybe he was just helping out the boss while she was fixing up his house in anticipation of the day Maggie would move in with him.

Phoebe wished she had someone to talk to about it. She was afraid that if she broached the subject to her mother, her mom would remind her that Richie had a girlfriend and that she was wasting her time. And if she brought up the subject with Mavis, Mavis would remind her that she'd already had one bad experience with a man and when was she going to learn? And she couldn't talk to her kids about it, because adults didn't ask kids for advice, and even if she did, she got the feeling that they were becoming as attached to Richie as she was.

Worst of all, she couldn't talk about it to the one person who was becoming her best friend, because he was the person in question.

DORY WAS GETTING WORRIED that maybe she should have told her mother that Dad was going to visit them. But what if she told her and her mom got upset and then Dad changed his mind and didn't come after all? Then it would mean that she had upset her mom for no reason.

She thought the best thing to do would be to call her father at school. She didn't know how much a call to New Jersey would cost, but when they pooled their money together, she and Ben had almost ten dollars in coins. She was sure that would be enough. Ben didn't like giving up his money, but Dory convinced him that their father would return the money to them when they saw him. She wasn't sure that was true, because Dad had never been one to hand out money, but she had heard from one of the girls in her class whose parents were divorced that divorced fathers were much more generous with money than married fathers.

After school on Tuesday she and Ben walked down to the nearest public phone, which was in a booth outside a gas station, and there she called Information, got the phone number for the university, then called the school's office. When she was told her father was in a class, she told the woman speaking that it was an emergency, a matter of life or death, and the woman told her to hold on.

Dory was afraid her money would all be gone before her father got to the phone, but the woman must have believed her about it being an emergency, because her dad was on the phone pretty fast.

"Hi, Dad," she said when he answered.

"Dory? Is that you? Are you and Ben all right?"

"We're fine, Dad." She held out the phone to Ben and told him to say hi, and after he had, she said, "I just said it was an emergency because I didn't have enough change to call you a second time."

"Did you get my letter, honey?"

"That's why I'm calling. Just when exactly are you visiting us?"

"I thought I'd pick you up around noon on Saturday, if it's all right with your mother."

"Okay, that's fine. We'll see you then, Dad."

"It is all right with your mother, isn't it?"

Dory sighed. "What I was thinking, Dad, since Mom won't even be there and Richie already knows—"

"*Richie?* Who's Richie?"

"Mom's deputy."

"Your mother's *what*?"

"She was elected sheriff. Didn't you hear?"

"She was *what*?"

The operator came on and said something about Dory's time being up, and Dory, before she could be disconnected, yelled into the phone, "We'll see you Saturday, Dad," and then hung up, and they ran all the way home in case she owed more money and the telephone company was coming after her.

She was sure that her mom would be at Richie's house well before noon, which would mean, if they just went out to eat with their dad and then came right home, Mom wouldn't even have to know about it. Unless Richie told her. But she didn't think he would. He seemed like the type who could keep a secret.

She couldn't think of anything else they could do with their dad anyway. He wouldn't know how long a drive it was to go to a movie, and it didn't seem right, somehow, to go to a movie when her mom couldn't go.

She wanted to see her dad because she missed him, even though, in a way, she blamed him a lot for breaking up the family. But she was sorry that she wasn't going to be able to help Richie on Saturday. She had loved helping him with the closet, and on Sunday he had let her do all the measurements for the pantry and she was given a chance to show him how good she was at fractions.

Still, she hadn't seen her dad in a long time and Richie would be around for a while. At least, she hoped he would, and she thought her mother hoped so, too.

Dory just hoped that whatever her mother had done wrong with her father, she wouldn't do the same thing with Richie.

THURSDAY WAS THE ONLY EVENTFUL DAY at the office, and it came at the right time, because by Thursday both Phoebe and Richie were getting tired of endlessly discussing what work they were going to do on their houses, while at the same time having to sit in the office instead of being able to do it.

What was surprising was that they hadn't gotten on each other's nerves sooner, but by noon on Thursday, they were reaching that point.

Phoebe was reading the mail aloud.

What had surprised her at first was that the sheriff's department got junk mail just like everyone else. She had just finished reading to him how much they'd win in the Publisher's Clearinghouse Sweepstakes. The next envelope offered up something more interesting. So interesting, that she read it to herself first before looking over at Richie and saying, "This is interesting."

Richie gave her a look that said he was waiting for the punch line.

"I'm serious, it is interesting. We're invited to join other Vermont law officers in a weekend in prison."

"They have that every year," Richie said, sounding bored.

"What's it like?" she asked him.

"How would I know? We never went."

"You passed up an opportunity like that?"

He laughed, obviously thinking she was kidding. "Yeah, we managed to miss it."

"I think it was your duty to go. How else can you know what the people you lock up go through?"

"Billy knew what they went through. They go through a dry spell, that's what, and Billy doesn't believe in giving up drinking."

"I'm not Billy."

"I've noticed."

"I think they have a point," Phoebe said.

"Listen, my dear sheriff, if you want to go get yourself locked up, be my guest."

"I think we should both be their guests."

"If I wanted to spend time in prison, Phoebe, I'd go commit a crime."

"I'm going to send in this application for the whole department, and that means both of us."

"What about your kids? You going to bring them along, too?"

"They can stay with my mother. This is a worthwhile thing, Richie, and it'll give me a chance to learn something practical about law enforcement."

"That's nonsense and you know it. If you want a vacation, go to Bermuda."

"It's not a vacation and I think it's our duty to go. I'm going to fill in your name," she said, already having filled in hers.

He already had his mouth open to answer her, when the phone rang, and instead he said, "Sheriff's department," into the receiver.

She listened, but all he said was, "Yes, okay, right away, yeah, we'll be there," and then hung up.

"We have work?" Phoebe asked, hoping that they did.

"The library's reporting a flasher in their parking lot and want us to check it out."

"A flasher? In Greensboro Bend?"

"It is a little hard to believe," Richie admitted, "but don't knock it. It'll at least get us out of the office."

Phoebe was already getting into her jacket and putting on her hat, and had to yell at Richie to hurry it up.

"What do you think, he's got a getaway car there?" he asked, taking his time.

"I want him, Richie. He'll be my first arrest."

"All right, take it easy," he said, but she was already out the door. She was eager to prove herself and this time she was going to do it right. She knew she goofed with Gladys, but she also knew she learned from her mistakes. There was not going to be a chase across the snow with this prisoner.

She had the car started by the time Richie got in, and as soon as she pulled away from the curb she put the siren on. She had been dying to use it officially.

"What the hell do you think you're doing?" he yelled at her over the sound of the siren.

"We're on our way to the scene of a crime, aren't we?"

He reached out and turned off the siren. "You think he's just going to stand around and wait for you when he hears the siren? Haven't you ever heard of sneaking up on someone?"

"I just wanted to put a scare into him. Maybe if he hears the siren he won't flash anyone else."

When she pulled the car into the parking lot and skidded to a stop, a man in a brown overcoat began to run out of the lot. "We're in time," she said. "There he is."

"What're you going to do next?" Richie asked.

"Don't just sit there, go after him."

Richie grinned over at her. "And if he runs?"

"He's twice your age, Richie. If he runs, catch him."

"Why don't you go after him, Phoebe, and I'll go in the library and talk to the witnesses."

"I don't have a gun," Phoebe mumbled.

"What was that? I didn't hear you clearly."

"I said I didn't have a gun. You might have to shoot into the air to get him to stop, like you did with Gladys."

"Do I hear you advocating the use of a gun?"

"Damn it, Richie, he's going to get away while you're arguing."

"All right, calm down. Go on in the library while I get him."

Phoebe, who was suddenly wishing she had a gun so she could do the capturing, went inside the library. With the exception of the librarian, the only person there was a woman of vintage years.

"You're the new sheriff, aren't you?" asked the librarian, a younger woman but still getting on in years.

"Yes," Phoebe said. "I believe you called us?"

"It's a pleasure meeting you. I voted for you, you know."

"Thank you," Phoebe said, not entirely meaning it. "I believe you reported a flasher?"

The woman nodded. "Mrs. Donovan over there saw him. Clear as day, right in the parking lot. You would think he would have picked a better spot than the library."

Phoebe would've thought so too. She couldn't imagine what the flasher had in mind flashing an elderly woman, whom she now saw used a cane. Mrs. Donovan was slowly approaching the counter.

Phoebe met her halfway. "I'm the sheriff, Mrs. Donovan. Could you tell me what happened?"

"A dirty old man flashed me—that's what happened," said the woman in a loud voice. Due, no doubt, to the hearing aid in her ear.

Phoebe felt herself blush. If it had been her, she would no doubt have been too embarrassed to report it. Or she would have felt in some way responsible for having been the one to be flashed in the first place. "Can you describe him?" she asked.

"Which part of him would you like me to describe?"

Feeling her blush deepening, Phoebe said, "What was he wearing?"

But instead of answering her, the woman gazed past her, and Phoebe turned around in time to see Richie walking in with the culprit.

"That's him," shouted Mrs. Donovan, and the librarian said, "Oh, my," and Phoebe noted the amused look on Richie's face and wished he'd wipe it off. This was no time for levity.

"You positively identify him?" Phoebe asked. She had heard that line used on TV cop shows.

"I certainly do," the woman said.

Richie seemed to be waiting for Phoebe to say more, but she didn't know what came next. As though knowing this, Richie said, "You'll need to come with us to city hall, ma'am, and make a statement."

"I will not ride in the same car with that pervert," said Mrs. Donovan. "I'll follow you in my car."

The librarian seemed sorry to see them go, and Phoebe had an idea she had welcomed the excitement as much as she had.

"Where's city hall?" Phoebe asked Richie on the way to the car.

"That's where Daryl works," Richie said. "What did you think that was?"

Hating to appear stupid in front of a criminal, Phoebe didn't ask any further questions. When Richie got into the back seat with the man, though, Phoebe said, "Make sure he's handcuffed."

"He's not going anywhere," Richie said.

"That's exactly what I thought about Gladys. Just follow the proper procedure, Richie. Please."

She was halfway back to the office, driving slowly so Mrs. Donovan could follow, when she heard whispering going on in the back seat.

Then Richie said, "I believe we made a mistake, Sheriff."

"What was that?"

"He wasn't flashing her."

"Richie, we have a witness."

"Phoebe, I've known Wally for a long time and I tend to believe him."

"He'll get his chance to say that in court."

"I'm no flasher, lady," said the accused.

Phoebe ignored him. She was sure that law officials heard this kind of thing every day.

"I was relieving myself."

"Did I hear him correctly?" she asked Richie, hoping neither of them could see her blush in the rearview mirror.

There was more whispering, and then Richie said, "He was relieving himself in the bushes behind the library, when this car drove in and almost hit him. It scared him, so he turned around before he had time to—"

"That's his story," Phoebe interrupted, not wanting to believe him because she had wanted to make her first arrest.

"Phoebe, this is going to cost the county a lot of money for nothing. I say we give him a ride home."

"Could we talk about this, Richie?"

"Phoebe, this is ridiculous."

Phoebe put her directional signal on and pulled over to the side of the road. Good sense prevailed over glory. "All right, Richie, let him go, but I'm not driving him home."

The door opened and she saw the man get out, and the next thing she knew Mrs. Donovan was pounding on her window with her cane.

Phoebe rolled down the window. "I'm sorry, Mrs. Donovan, but it seems the man wasn't flashing you after all. He was relieving himself behind the library when you pulled in, and you surprised him, that's all."

Mrs. Donovan looked furious. "Isn't that against the law?"

Phoebe turned around for Richie's opinion.

"Technically, yes," said Richie, "but it's not worth putting him in jail for. The judge'll just say we're wasting his time and let him go."

"I'm sorry, Mrs. Donovan, but I think it was a misunderstanding," Phoebe told her. "But we appreciate good citizens like you reporting in to us."

Mrs. Donovan didn't look mollified. "You're as bad as Billy Benson," Phoebe was told, but at least Mrs. Donovan returned to her car.

"I hope that's not true," Phoebe said.

Richie got in the front seat beside her. "Billy wouldn't have even bothered with a flasher."

"I was really hoping to make an arrest," Phoebe admitted to him.

"I know you were, but hang in there. You'll be able to make plenty of them this summer."

"Do we have a jail?"

"We have one cell."

"Why haven't I ever seen it?"

Richie sighed. "I'll take you for a tour when we get back, okay? But on one condition."

"What's that?"

"That you don't redecorate it."

MAVIS WAS LEADING a double life and it was making a nervous wreck of her.

By day she was the guiding light of the Crazy Quilt Women's Commune; by night she was sneaking off to see Noggie.

Next to her father, he was the most intelligent man she had ever met. And the only man she'd met since her first year of college who hadn't been intimidated by her mind. Intellectually he appeared to be her equal; socially, however, he lagged way behind.

"Baby doll, you came to see your Noggie," he said to her the first time she showed up at his tent.

With a grimace at his choice of words, she let herself be led inside. "See, Noggie? You say you're a feminist, but then you call me your 'baby doll.' How would you like it if I called you that?"

"Call me whatever comes to mind, you little vixen."

Mavis shook her head. "Just listen to you. 'Little.' 'Doll.' I thought you didn't believe in people defining other people by their size?"

Noggie grinned. "Take off your clothes and let's get acquainted."

"Noggie, either you treat me with respect, as your equal, or I'm walking right out of here."

"I only meant your jacket."

"I got a cold the other night. I'd rather leave it on."

"Oh, you've been sick," Noggie said. "I wondered why you hadn't come to see me sooner."

"Let's get one thing straight," Mavis said. "I didn't come to see you because I enjoyed being attacked in the snow. Women don't like having kisses forced on them, Noggie. If I hadn't thought there was a chance that you could be redeemed, I never would have stopped by."

"Nonsense. Don't try my intelligence." He pounced on her and pulled her down to the floor of the tent. "First we'll make out a little bit. Then we'll have a discussion."

PHOEBE HADN'T BEEN HOME ten minutes on Friday, when Richie showed up at the door.

"Did I forget something?" she asked him, while behind her the kids were calling out greetings.

Richie grinned at her, then looked past her to the children. "Come on, we're going to the movies."

That was a sneaky thing to say, because now she'd be the bad guy when she said no. "Richie, there's no way I'm driving to Burlington in the middle of a snowstorm."

"Get your jackets and let's go," Richie said. "The movies are at my house."

"We haven't even eaten yet," she protested.

"That's all taken care of," Richie said, and Phoebe saw that Ben and Dory were all ready to go.

Shaking her head, she put her own jacket back on. "I suppose you mean television," she said, but not really minding the idea.

"Not at all. We're going to watch my favorite movie of all time."

He refused to say anything more about it, though, until they got to his house. Then he showed them all the new VCR he had bought. "The stuff on TV's so lousy and it's so far to drive to a movie, so I thought I'd start renting them."

While the kids were esconced before the television, Richie cooked them all hamburgers and fries and even popped some popcorn, since, as he said, what was a movie without popcorn?

"I hope we're not going to have to sit through some Disney movie," Phoebe said, getting out milk for the kids.

"Would I do that to you?" Richie asked.

"Probably."

"What you're going to see is the funniest movie about a sheriff that was ever made."

"*Blazing Saddles*," Phoebe guessed.

"You've seen it."

"Once, but I loved it. I wouldn't mind seeing it again. Only, as I recall, it wasn't exactly suited to children."

"Nonsense. As I recall there wasn't one thing adult about that movie."

"There was sex."

"Sex? I don't remember sex."

"I think there was," Phoebe said. "I remember the language, though. The language was adult."

"Anything your kids haven't heard before?"

"They haven't heard it from me."

"Not to worry," Richie said. "The VCR comes with a remote control and whenever there's bad language, I'll just zap it forward."

"By then they'll have heard it."

"I'll anticipate it."

Phoebe gave up protesting. The kids would love the movie, particularly since she, too, was a sheriff. And a night out with someone else cooking was heaven.

As a concession to the kids, who appeared to be riveted to the nightly news, they served the food in the living room. By the time the news was over, they were finished eating, and then it was like one of Phoebe's daydreams coming true. She and Richie sat at either end of the couch with the kids between them, and Richie started the movie.

She had forgotten about the first scene around the campfire, which she had always found rather gross, but the children were convulsed with laughter and she couldn't help joining in.

True to his word, Richie zapped any objectionable words, but instead of fooling the kids, they merely yelled out the words they'd been deprived of hearing.

And when the sheriff appeared, Ben got so excited he stood up.

"Look, he's got a horse," he yelled. "Why don't you have a horse, Mom?"

"Because this isn't the West."

"She also can't ride," Dory observed.

By the end of the movie Ben was practicing drawing an imaginary gun and Dory was asking why they didn't have a VCR. Phoebe was wishing they had a reason to stay longer.

Richie provided that reason. "And now," he said, "for the adults."

"Oh, great, a boring movie," Dory said, guessing before Phoebe what was coming.

"You rented two movies?" Phoebe asked.

"Another oldie but goodie," Richie said, getting up and switching the tapes.

She knew what it was the moment it began. "*Casablanca*," she said, not able to keep the pleasure out of her voice.

"I suppose it's a love story," Dory said.

"The very best," said Richie, which had been exactly what Phoebe had been about to say.

"What a perfect double feature," she said, catching Richie's glance and holding it for a moment. Being this close to him and not being alone was driving her crazy.

"I figured you were a closet romantic," he said.

Of course she was, and feeling more and more like coming out of the closet. "I didn't figure you were," she said.

"I'm not—I got the movie for you," said Richie, but if that wasn't a romantic gleam in his eyes she was very much mistaken.

"Can we have a little quiet during the movie?" Dory asked.

Twenty minutes into the movie Ben was asleep from boredom. The way Phoebe had it figured, Dory would be next, and then she and Richie would carry them into his bedroom and let them sleep while they enjoyed the rest of the movie. Alone. Together. Maybe very close together.

It didn't work out that way. Dory was as clearly entranced with the story as they were, and "entranced" was the word, even though Phoebe was sure she'd seen it at least a dozen times before. Her pragmatic daughter even had tears in her eyes at the end.

"This has been great," Phoebe said when Richie was rewinding the movie. "I've really enjoyed myself."

Richie gave her the kind of look that said she would have enjoyed herself even more if they'd had some privacy. "Tomorrow night's Clint Eastwood night," he said.

"My brother loves Clint Eastwood," Dory said.

"Those movies are much too violent," Phoebe objected.

Richie grinned at her. "Not the two I got. They're the ones with chimps in them."

"Are we invited?" Dory asked.

"I didn't pick out the chimp ones for me," Richie said, winking at Phoebe.

Phoebe got up. "I'll do the dishes before we go." She thought maybe Dory would take a nap and Richie would join her in the kitchen.

But Richie said, "Forget it, it only takes a minute in the dishwasher."

"Well, if you really want us over again tomorrow night, I'll bring the food."

"I'll take you up on that offer."

"It'll be spaghetti," Dory said. "We always have spaghetti on Saturday nights."

"My favorite," Richie said. "If it's made right."

"It's made right," Phoebe asserted.

Dory was up and stretching. "We better go, Mom, if you're going to get up in the morning."

"Not too early," Phoebe said.

"Aren't you going to finish painting his kitchen?"

"I don't have to get up at the crack of dawn to do that."

"Well, I feel like getting to bed," said Dory, who then exchanged a look with Richie, making Phoebe wonder what they were up to.

Her suspicions were ridiculous because they couldn't possibly be up to anything. It was probably just that Dory was looking forward to working with Richie again.

That was really the only thing wrong with the exchange of work: she didn't get to see Richie while she did it.

Then Richie said, "Why don't you go get your brother up, Dory," and the second Dory left the room, he and Phoebe practically flew into each other's arms and there was time for one, frustrating kiss before they heard the kids in the hall. One frustrating kiss was better than none at all, though.

Dory surprised Phoebe by giving Richie a kiss on the cheek when they left and also thanking him. Since no one in her family ever kissed anyone else on the cheek, Phoebe wondered where she got it from. Wherever, it was rather nice.

Phoebe didn't kiss him on the cheek. Instead she just remembered that only seconds ago they had been clinging together and merely said, "See you in the morning, but not too early."

"I think we've all forgotten something," Richie said. "You came in my car."

And so there was the drive home and good-nights all over again, and Dory did some whispering with Richie before she got out of the car.

After Phoebe got Ben to bed, Dory said, "I need to talk to you, Mom."

"Can't it wait until morning, honey?"

"I don't think so. Richie said I should tell you, and I think he's right. Don't be mad at me, though, okay?"

"Now you've got me worried."

The last thing she had expected to hear from her daughter was that Ted was going to arrive the next day. "Of course I don't mind, Dory. I never meant for you not to see your father." Although if he had been her idea of a good father he wouldn't have waited so long.

"We're just going to lunch with him, Mom."

"Darling, it's all right." And with Richie there, she wouldn't even have to see him.

"He sounded really surprised when I said you were sheriff. I don't think he believed me."

"I'll bet he didn't," Phoebe said. In Ted's opinion she wasn't capable of giving an order. But maybe that was because she had always left that to him. If so, she was changing. Just ask Richie.

"What if he wants us to visit him or something?" Dory asked.

"Honey, if you want to visit him on your vacations, that's perfectly all right. I know you love your father."

"I love you more."

"You don't have to take sides, Dory. You can love us both."

"You didn't leave me."

"He didn't, either. He left me, and I wouldn't let him have you."

"That's not the way I see it, Mom. But if he wants us to visit, do we have to?"

"No. Only if you want to."

Phoebe almost wished she hadn't been told. She didn't want to see Ted again; she didn't even want to hear his name. But it didn't do any good pretending he didn't exist, because he could show up and want to see the kids, and she knew she couldn't refuse him that.

She realized that somewhere along the way she had stopped loving him. It had probably been sooner than she thought, but the betrayal had lasted longer. Now she didn't even feel that anymore, except for the children's sake.

She felt lonely at times, but she had felt lonely at times when she was married. What she thought she missed the most was the companionship. She had realized that tonight when the four of them had watched the movie. It had reminded her of when she was married, except that she had felt freer to voice her own opinions.

But that hadn't been Ted's fault; that had been hers. For some reason she had always been intimidated by Ted—probably because he was smarter than she was. She didn't feel that way with Richie. For all she knew he might be more intelligent than her, too, but that wasn't going to stop her from having her own opinions and standing by them.

Hearing about Ted had somehow spoiled the evening. Instead of going to bed and thinking about what a good time she had had with Richie, instead she'd be thinking about Ted showing up after all this time.

And finding his ex-wife was a sheriff.

Chapter Twelve

Richie was hoping Dory had taken his advice and told Phoebe that her ex-husband was going to show up. He didn't think it would be the kind of surprise anyone would appreciate. Bad surprises usually weren't. And it had to be a bad surprise. When someone walks out on you you usually aren't eager for that person's company.

He was pretty sure that was the case, anyway. One indication was that Phoebe rarely alluded to her marriage or her ex. And on the occasions when she did it was matter-of-factly. He knew the kids were trying to protect her, that they thought the news would make her cry, but he wasn't at all sure of that. He thought she could handle it. And the reason he thought that was he thought the two of them had something special going. Something special enough to make her forget all about her ex, just the way it made him forget all about Maggie.

He had enjoyed the night before. Of course he would have enjoyed it even more if they had been alone, but he liked her kids. He thought staying home in his own house, where it was warm and snug, where it wasn't noisy and crowded and smoky, was a lot better than hanging out in a bar. Maybe not when he was alone. Then he preferred a bar. But when he had good company there was no place like home.

Phoebe and her kids were good company. Phoebe was even good company without her kids, making his job a lot more interesting than it had been with Billy. The kids were an added attraction, though, and he enjoyed the hell out of them. He couldn't wait to spend another evening watching movies with them. In anticipation of this—and because Phoebe was going to provide the food this time—he had driven into town and stocked up on candy bars and another can of popcorn. And while he was there he had gotten a third movie at the rental place. He figured the kids might last through the two Clint Eastwood ones, and the third was strictly for Phoebe and him.

He wondered if it would shock her or make her nervous. He wondered if it would make him nervous. It wasn't as though it were a dirty movie or anything like that, but it did have an R rating and he had heard it was pretty sexy. And he had heard it from Daryl, so he believed it.

Of course, his plans would go right down the drain if it turned out Dory outlasted two movies, although he thought the kid was knowledgeable enough to take a hint and go to bed by that time. And if she wasn't he'd just return the movie unseen, that was all. It wasn't as though the movies were costing him an arm and a leg. All five of them could see two movies for about the same price it would cost for one person to go to a movie theater and see one. In fact, less when you counted the price of the gas.

Funny, but he'd never thought of getting a VCR or renting movies with Maggie. Maggie always liked to go out, see people, keep on the move. Maggie was young. He had been like that at her age, too, so he could understand it. But after years of going out, seeing people and keeping on the move, it got more and more of a pleasure just to stay home.

Oh, hell, who was he kidding? It was Phoebe who made it more of a pleasure; it had nothing to do with age. And for all he knew, Phoebe might prefer going out. After being married all those years she might be tired of staying home.

The problem was, there weren't too many places he could take her out to with the kids along. In the summer there would be. In the summer they could go to the lake or go for drives or just walk in the woods. He supposed they could all go skiing. Only skiing was an expensive hobby, plus he couldn't ski, and he had no desire to learn, because skiing always entailed, somewhere along the line, a broken leg. He could live his entire life without ever really wanting a broken leg.

He was looking forward to building Phoebe a pantry. She had a little back porch, a useless thing, since if you opened the door you fell into the snow because there weren't any steps. All she used it for was a trash can, and later he could build her an outdoor container for the trash can. It was the perfect size for a pantry.

He was going to miss having the kids around today and he was also going to miss Dory's help. But at least their father didn't visit often; he would hate it if he had them every weekend. In fact, it looked as though he visited about once a year. Richie figured that was enough. If their father really wanted to see them, he wouldn't have left them. Richie had seen men who had left their families and then started seeing their kids on weekends, buying them presents, spending lots of money on them, as though trying to prove what great fathers they were. He hated that. And all it ever seemed to do was confuse the kids.

It was good they were coming over to his place tonight. That way Phoebe wouldn't have time to brood about her ex and the kids wouldn't have time to brood about their father's visit. They'd have a good time, share a few laughs and get back to normal.

"DON'T MAKE A BIG PRODUCTION over seeing him," Dory was coaching Ben.

"I don't know what that means, Dory."

"Just don't act excited and throw yourself all over him. Just act cool, that's all. I mean, it's about time he came to visit us, don't you think?"

She knew Ben, though; he'd probably act like a little puppy dog when he saw Dad. Dory wasn't even going to kiss him. He could kiss her if he wanted, she wouldn't stop him, but she wasn't going to start it, either.

"Don't forget to get our money back," Ben said.

"I won't. And Ben, when Mom asks us if we had a good time, don't start raving about it and saying how great it was."

"It might not be great."

"Just remember, we don't want her to feel bad."

"I know that, Dory."

"Okay, I'll put some water on to boil and you wake Mom up. Richie ought to be here any minute."

WHEN RICHIE GOT THERE it was a relief to find out that Phoebe did know about it, and since it was after eleven by then, she was going to stick around and see her ex when he arrived. He had known she wasn't the type to run over to his house and hide out.

Dory seemed a lot more nervous than her mother. She kept going from the kitchen, where Phoebe and Richie were having coffee, to the living room window to look outside. Ben was his usual self, asking a stream of questions about the movies they were going to see that night.

Richie found himself wondering, for the first time, what her ex was like. Whatever he was like would give Richie some indication of what Phoebe liked in a man. He knew one thing about him, and that was that he taught at Princeton. That was something Richie couldn't ever match, even if he wanted to. He had gone to a community college for two years, and that was enough schooling as far as he was concerned.

Well, her ex had to be a pretty good man, or Phoebe wouldn't have liked him and the kids wouldn't have turned out so well. Because they were good kids. Dory might be a little quiet and Ben might be a little talkative, but put them both in the same room and things worked out perfectly.

He and Phoebe were sitting there, real calm, talking about the pantry, but when Dory came in to say that her father had arrived, tension filled the air like smoke. He could almost breathe it.

Ben immediately ran to the door and Richie could hear Dory telling him to calm down. Richie felt like telling Phoebe to calm down, but didn't feel it was his place to do so. For once she wasn't blushing. Instead she had gone a little pale, and even though he knew she was cutting down on the cigarettes, intending to cut them out completely, she reached for one immediately and seemed to gain back a little of her color with the first puff.

He wondered if he would ever do something that would make her reach for a cigarette like that. He hoped not.

He could hear the front door being opened and he wondered when Phoebe was going to get up and go greet her ex. Then it occurred to him that the ex would almost certainly misinterpret Richie sitting there at the kitchen table having coffee. In the morning. He was pretty sure the ex would think he had spent the night.

He was about to suggest that to Phoebe, then decided she had enough on her mind.

Then Phoebe got up, and when she went to the door of the living room, Richie followed behind her. She just might be in need of some moral support.

He saw Dory tentatively eyeing her father and Ben holding back, then rushing into the man's arms. The man was mostly bald, which delighted Richie no end. Maybe it was his Indian blood, but the men in his family always kept their hair.

And then, and he didn't know why he hadn't seen her sooner, he saw a woman behind Phoebe's ex, and he realized he'd had the bad taste to bring along the new wife. The pregnant new wife, at least by several months, but carrying it well.

He saw that Phoebe had already noticed her and had gone pale again, but then suddenly everyone was talking at once. Ted was introducing his wife as Deedee; Ben had run upstairs and returned with his cat, whom he was thrusting at his father, who didn't appear to like cats and was telling Ben to take the cat away; Deedee was saying something about where was spring and what a lot of snow they still had; Phoebe was trying to introduce Richie, only no one was paying any attention; and Dory was the only one being quiet, watching everyone, because even Richie had introduced himself to the ex by then.

Phoebe said, "Wouldn't you like to sit down for a few minutes before you go? I can fix coffee."

The ex, Ted, said, "I've cut out caffeine," and Deedee nodded in agreement, but everyone took a seat in the living room. It was Ted and Deedee on the couch, Phoebe in the rocking chair, Ben on the floor with his cat, Dory standing by her mother's chair, and Richie finally carried in a kitchen chair and made himself comfortable.

Ted was looking at Richie and saying, "I didn't quite catch your name."

"That's mom's deputy, Richie," Ben said.

Ted had the look of an aging preppy and the voice to match. "Dory said something like that on the phone, but I thought I was mistaken. What's this all about, Phoebe?"

Phoebe shrugged. "I'm the new sheriff," she said, as though things like that happened to her every day.

With a smile showing his small, even teeth, Ted said, "I didn't know you had an interest in that sort of thing." And when no one said anything, he said, "I think it's fine, though."

When still no one said anything, Richie took pity on him and said, "I hear you're up here to do some skiing."

Ted nodded. "I wanted to see the children, and I thought as long as we were going to be near Stowe, we might as well take advantage of it."

Then there was another silence, which Richie didn't feel like filling, and Phoebe finally said, "What time will you be bringing them back, Ted?"

"I'll have them back by dinnertime, Phoebe."

Ben spoke up. "We're going to have spaghetti at Richie's house and watch two movies."

The cat, in the way of all cats, was now on his feet and rubbing against Ted's trousers, picking out the one person in the room who had displayed a dislike for him. As though afraid the cat would next jump into his lap, Ted stood up and said, "Well, if you kids are ready, I know we could eat some lunch."

The kids, who hadn't finished breakfast that long ago, were polite enough not to say so. Ben and Dory put on their jackets and Richie shook Ted's hand and nodded to Deedee, and as soon as they were out of the door, Richie heard himself breathing a sigh of relief.

Then he heard a distinct sob, followed by another, and when he turned around he saw Phoebe dissolving in tears.

Oh, hell, he thought, *she still cares for him.* If there was one thing he hated to see it was someone crying over someone else who wasn't worth it. He turned and took her hands, which she was using to cover her face, and put them around his neck, and then he put his arms around her and hoped he was coming off looking comforting and not as though he was taking advantage of the situation. Which he wasn't.

"Hey, come on, don't feel so bad. You saw him and it's over and the earth didn't cave in, did it? It just takes time, that's all."

"It's not him. I'm not crying over him."

"Yeah, it wasn't too thoughtful of him to bring along the new wife, I can understand how you feel.

But, Phoebe, you have nothing to be jealous about. The only thing she's got going for her is youth. You're worth ten of her."

"But she's having a baby," she said, her sobbing increasing.

He couldn't think of anything to say to that, because obviously Deedee was having a baby.

"I could kill him," Phoebe said, her crying temporarily diminishing and then reviving again.

"I could kill him, too, Phoebe, for making you so unhappy. But he's not worth it. He's not even worth your crying."

"You don't understand," she said, moving her face off his shoulder. "She's having a baby and I'm not. He wouldn't let me have another one."

"You mean you're unhappy because she's pregnant and you're not?"

Phoebe nodded. "He said two were enough, that he could only afford to educate two properly. I would've liked five, and now he's going to have three and I'm only going to have two."

He put his finger under her chin and lifted up her face so that he could see her. "You can still have kids, Phoebe. It's not like you're too old or anything. And anyone who can have as good kids as Ben and Dory shouldn't stop with two."

The tears stopped flowing and settled in her eyes. "It's not that easy, Richie. Not too many men want a woman with two kids, and I think children need a father."

"Well, sure, I didn't mean just to have them on your own. But hell, Phoebe, any guy would be lucky to get you and those kids of yours."

"You really think so?"

"Sure I do. I'd probably say it anyway just to make you feel better, but I mean it." And then for no other reason except that he felt like it, he moved his head down a little and started to kiss her. It must have taken her as much by surprise as it did him, because for a moment or two she didn't even move her lips, but then she was moving in closer to him and kissing him back, and he stopped thinking about anything and just enjoyed the way he was feeling.

THEY WERE SITTING in a nice restaurant with real tablecloths and napkins that Dory had never been in before. She had already brought up the subject of the money for the phone call when they had been in the car, and her dad had said, "Sure, Dory," but he hadn't reached right in his pocket and given it to her, so now she was going to order the most expensive things on the menu so in case he didn't pay her she wouldn't get off free.

In the car her father had asked them lots of questions about school and they had answered him, but none of it had seemed real. It used to be their father knew what teachers they were talking about and what they were studying in school, but now he no longer knew and he didn't even seem particularly interested. It was more like he was just being polite, which made him seem not like a father at all.

Ben, who had not acted shy with him at all when he first arrived, was now being very quiet and stealing glances at their father and his new wife. Dory didn't know what she thought of Deedee, because she didn't say much and seemed even shyer than Ben. She supposed she was good-looking in a way, but nothing special. She wondered what it was about her that made her father leave them for her.

"This Richie," said their father, "he looks like a nice guy."

"Yes," Ben agreed, and Dory didn't say anything. She didn't want to discuss Richie behind his back. That wouldn't be fair.

"It's nice seeing your mother getting out and having a career," he tried next, and this time Deedee spoke for the first time.

"I thought you said she liked being a housewife," she said to their father.

Her father didn't say anything to that and there was a long, uncomfortable silence, and Dory finally asked Deedee, "Do you want a boy or a girl?"

"A boy," said Deedee, and Dory instantly hated her. She could see Ben's lower lip begin to tremble with the knowledge that his dad was going to have another son who would probably take his place.

Dory didn't think it was a very good idea seeing their father. It wasn't turning out as she'd thought. They were all acting like strangers and her dad was acting more like he was doing his duty than enjoying it. That was too bad, because he had been a good father, but now he seemed to have forgotten how.

Even if he remembered, things would never be the same again. Because of him they were living in a little house in Vermont with an unhappy mother... except that wasn't really the truth any longer. Lately her mother had changed. She hadn't changed back to what she had been in New Jersey, but instead had changed into something even better. Dory figured it was mostly being sheriff and maybe partly because of Richie.

Dory had the thought that maybe her father had realized something her mother was only just realizing, and that was that maybe they were never the right person for each other. Her mother seemed to laugh more and have a better time with Richie than she had ever had with their father.

She looked across the table at Deedee, who was looking very uncomfortable. Maybe her father and Deedee also laughed and had a good time but weren't doing it now because of Ben and her.

Hoping that her mom wouldn't mind, Dory told them the story about her mother and Richie taking Gladys to the prison. She saw Deedee's eyes kind of light up, and then she heard her father chuckle, and pretty soon everyone was laughing and things seemed friendlier. Even Ben started acting normal, asking lots of questions, and Dory began to think that even though her father would never really be like a father to her anymore, maybe they could be friends. And maybe, after a while, her mother could be friends with him, too.

Then she had another thought. "Your baby will be our sister or brother," she said to Deedee.

Deedee nodded. "You'll have to come visit after it's born."

"We don't have a very big place," said their father, and Dory said, "Neither do we, but it's okay."

And after that there weren't any more long silences.

NOT WANTING TO BE ALONE, Phoebe had stayed at home and helped Richie build the pantry. She didn't do any of the actual work, but she handed him tools and cleaned up the messes he made and fixed them snacks when they got hungry.

Phoebe had opened up to him a little, telling him something about her marriage. At one point he said, "Does he have a sense of humor?"

Phoebe had to think about that and finally said, "Sometimes, but it's different from mine. I mean he'll tell jokes and he'll laugh at other people's jokes, but he doesn't have a sense of the ridiculous."

"That must have been hard on you," Richie said, "since you can act pretty ridiculous."

"Me? When do I act ridiculous?"

"All I can say, Phoebe, is that if Mel Brooks made a movie about you as sheriff, it would be funnier than *Blazing Saddles*."

"Do you also find Maggie ridiculous?" If he could ask about Ted, she should be able to ask about Maggie.

"Maggie has a good sense of humor."

Phoebe felt unaccountably jealous. She thought it was a good sign, a healthy sign. All of her emotions appeared to be coming back to her, and most of them were centered on Richie.

"How good is your sense of humor, Richie?"

"I'd say it's okay."

"Good enough to survive a fall off that ladder?"

He looked down at her and grinned. "Try it."

"I just may."

"You think I'd just take it lying down? What do you think I'd do to you in return?"

"Gee, Richie, you're scaring me to death."

"You don't think I can scare you?"

She was wishing he'd come down off the ladder and scare her, because she had a pretty good idea what that scare would entail. Kissing, that's what, and since she had enjoyed it before, she had every reason to believe she'd enjoy it a second time. She reached out and gave the ladder a shake.

"Keep it up, Phoebe."

She kept it up a little more, and he began to slowly climb down, his eyes never leaving hers. "I'm coming to get you," he said in a Jack Nicholson voice.

She started to back out of the porch into the kitchen, looking around for something to hit him with. The loaf of bread would do nicely, since it was soft white bread and wouldn't really hurt. She picked it up and began to swing it around.

"I get it," he said, standing in the doorway. "You're going to knock me down with that loaf of bread and have your way with me."

"You wish," Phoebe said, blushing because the thought had occurred to her.

"Go on, I'll make it easy for you," he said, sticking out his chin so that it was within her reach.

And because she wanted the reaction she knew she was going to get, she swung the loaf of bread into his chin, then followed it up by rushing into his arms. That was exactly where she wanted to be. In fact, she had thought of little else since the last time she had been there.

"The intrepid sheriff," he said, "running into dangerous situations."

"Go on, be dangerous."

"Make your day?"

"Yeah, make my day."

He gave her an altogether satisfying kiss, then said, "If we had all day, I probably would. But since your kids could show up at any minute, and they're too

Phoebe's Deputy

young for X-rated scenes, you'll just have to eat your heart out."

Phoebe fell totally and completely in love with him.

THE SPAGHETTI WASN'T GREAT. It was pure American spaghetti, if there was such a thing, as bland as a bologna sandwich on white bread. He ate it, though, and didn't complain, and waited for the day he could teach her how to make real spaghetti.

The kids had to be drawn out about their visit with their father. They were much more eager to talk about the movies they were going to see and maybe what movies they'd be invited to see the next week.

"We won't be here next week," Phoebe told them.

"Where are we going?" Ben asked.

"Yeah, where are you going?" Richie asked.

"Richie and I are going to be locked in prison next weekend," she told them.

"Leave me out of it," Richie said.

"What did you do?" Ben asked.

"We didn't do anything," Phoebe explained. "It's a program where law officers can learn what it's like to be locked up, that's all. I thought you could stay with Grandma."

"You actually call Katie Lou 'Grandma'?" he asked her.

"She's our grandma," Ben informed him.

"I think that sounds like a good idea," Dory said, eyeing her mother and Richie in a speculative manner that seemed too old for a kid her age.

"It's a rotten idea," Richie said. "Wouldn't you rather stay here and finish the pantry?"

"No."

"Grandma's got television," Ben said.

"Everyone has it but us," Dory said.

"I'm staying home and watching mine," Richie said.

Phoebe gave him an enticing smile. "Wouldn't you like a little vacation away from Greensboro Bend?"

"If that's your idea of a little vacation, go ahead. Just let me plan my own vacations." But he was already getting ideas from that enticing smile and knew he'd let himself be convinced any minute.

Although he'd be damned if any other woman could make a weekend spent in prison sound sexy.

Chapter Thirteen

"We'll never make it," Richie said for about the tenth time.

Phoebe was starting to agree with him. It was April, the rest of the country was being treated to spring weather, but here in Vermont they were in the middle of one of the season's worst blizzards. She could barely see a foot beyond the windshield, but turning back wouldn't improve anything. It was snowing just as hard behind them.

"It's bad enough your dragging me off to spend the weekend in prison," Richie said. "You don't have to get me killed, too."

"Are you dead, Richie?"

"Not yet."

"Then quit complaining."

"Just think, Phoebe, we could be over at my place, popping popcorn, watching a movie..."

"I didn't put a gun to your back. You agreed to go."

"I didn't know it was going to be under hazardous conditions."

The visibility went from a foot to zero and Phoebe slowed down to under five miles an hour. "It would be just as bad turning back."

"There's one consolation," Richie said. "We'll be the only ones who show up and they'll probably send us home."

"Be honest. Wouldn't you rather be locked up in a warm prison than driving in this storm?"

"Great choice you're giving me."

Phoebe was getting scared, but she didn't want to show it. She didn't want to give Richie any reason to say "I told you so," even if he had. The snow was now blowing across her windshield sideways and even the car was moving a little from the force of the wind. If there were somewhere to pull over and wait it out a little she would, but all she saw on all sides was just snow and more snow.

"If we had been smart," Richie said, "we would have told everyone we were going to this thing, but instead we would have headed straight for the sun."

"I don't think you take your profession very seriously."

"Let me know in ten years whether you still think going to prison makes for an enjoyable weekend."

"Where in the sun?"

"Anywhere where there's a beach and a few palm trees. It wouldn't have to be anything fancy."

Phoebe thought of lying on a beach with Richie, the warm sun beating down on her skin. All she could picture was the way she turned lobster red when out in the sun too long.

"Am I tempting you?" he asked.

"Not really."

For just a moment she had visibility and she saw a neon light up ahead on the right. She decided to pull in, whatever it was, and wait until the storm let up a little. She hoped it was a restaurant, as she wouldn't mind one last good meal before the prison fare they were going to be treated to.

"Was that a light I saw?" Richie asked.

"It looked like it. I'm going to pull in there."

"First sensible thing you've said."

By the time she had driven to where she had seen the light, she could no longer see it. She pulled over anyway. "I'm going to get out and see if there's somewhere to park."

"Let me go," Richie said, already opening the door.

She knew they didn't have a chance of reaching the prison unless some miracle occurred and the sun came out at night in Vermont. If it was a restaurant, though, or even a gas station, they could wait out the storm and then drive back home. She was disappointed, as she had been looking forward to getting away for the weekend. Not once, in fourteen years, had she ever been away by herself.

When Richie returned he said, "Yeah, there's a parking lot. Go up about six more yards, then turn right."

"What is it, a restaurant?"

"Not exactly."

But by that time she had pulled in, and for a moment clearly saw the motel sign. Motor Inn, it said, but she didn't feel like motoring into a motel. "Does it have a coffee shop?" she asked him.

"I don't know. All I was looking for was somewhere to get off the highway."

It wasn't his fault it was a motel instead of a restaurant, so she didn't complain. When she had parked next to a snow-covered car, she said, "Why don't you go in and find out if they have a restaurant?"

"Let's both go in," said Richie. "At least they'll have some heat on in the office."

Phoebe felt a little strange walking into a motel office with a man. It made her feel guilty, as though she were up to no good. But after she thought about that for a second, she realized it might be her only chance to be up to no good with Richie. They'd certainly never manage it with the kids around.

"What can I do for you folks?" asked the man behind the counter, without a trace of suspicion in his voice. Phoebe had been sure he would somehow know they weren't married.

"We could use some food," Richie told him.

"That's about the extent of the food," the man said, pointing to two machines against the wall in the lobby. One held soft drinks, the other candy bars.

"You're lucky," he continued, "I've only got one room left. Everyone's been pulling in here to get out of the storm. The radio says it's not going to stop until morning."

Richie looked over at Phoebe, and, surprisingly, she didn't blush. She had been sure she would blush. "I guess we better take it," she said.

"It seems like the only practical thing to do," Richie agreed.

She nodded, and he went about filling in the registration card as though he frequented motels every day. Maybe he did. He paid the man in advance, then asked for some change for the machine.

"Cokes and candy bars?" Phoebe asked.

"You have any other suggestions?"

"No. I'll have a Hershey with almonds."

"You got it," Richie said, feeding the coins in the machine.

Phoebe's Deputy

They had been told to bring nothing with them, as they wouldn't be allowed any personal possessions while in prison. Now Phoebe wished she'd ignored that. Her first night with Richie she would have appreciated having a nightgown, a toothbrush and her diaphragm.

They went down the covered walkway, past cars that were buried in snow, partially covered in snow and a couple, like theirs, still fairly snow free. Phoebe, looking down as she walked, had a view of some of the license plates. One of them made her look again, then stop dead in her tracks.

"What's the matter?" Richie asked.

"That's my sister's license plate," Phoebe said, recognizing the CQWC for Crazy Quilt Women's Commune.

He had already walked ahead and was putting the key in the door. "Come on, Phoebe. It's freezing out here."

She stared at the plate for a few more moments, then brushed a little snow off one fender. Light blue, the same color as Mavis's Chevy.

She went to the door of their room and looked in at Richie. "Richie, what could my sister possibly be doing at a motel?"

"Close the door, Phoebe. You're letting in cold air."

She closed the door and leaned back against it. The room had one bed, a color TV, no chairs—and her sister nearby. The last part made no sense at all.

"She's probably doing the same thing we're doing," Richie said.

"Mavis? Mavis hates men."

Richie gave her an amused look. "I was talking about getting out of the storm, Phoebe. What were you talking about?"

Phoebe didn't even blush. "Are you telling me, Richie Stuart, that you're planning on sleeping on the floor? I've been dying to make love with you for weeks, and now you're going to sleep on the floor?"

Richie couldn't contain his smile, although she could tell he made the effort. "You're dying to make love with me?"

"You didn't know?"

"Well, I knew I was dying to make love with you, but I wasn't positive it was mutual." He took off his jacket and hung it in the closet, all of his movements seeming like slow motion to her.

Phoebe took off hers, too, and hung it next to his. Then she sat down on the side of the bed and took off her boots. "It's not only mutual," she said, "but I think I better warn you about something first."

Richie sat down next to her and began to pull off his boots. "If you think you can scare me off, think again. I've been having X-rated thoughts about you since the first time I laid eyes on you."

X-rated thoughts sounded pretty exciting to Phoebe. She would have rated her own thoughts R rather than X, but that was because they were equal parts romance and sex. "The thing is, Richie, it's not just sex. I'm pretty sure I love you."

Richie began unbuttoning his shirt. "Pretty sure? That's a hell of a thing to say. I love you and I'm not afraid to say it."

Phoebe took off her wet socks and threw them in the direction of the radiator. He had now taken off his shirt, and she felt like burying her head in his chest.

She was so happy she was afraid to talk. She finally forced her eyes away from his chest and removed her hat. He was now unbuckling his belt.

"Cat got your tongue?" Richie asked. "Or are you afraid to just come out and say you love me?"

"I love you," she said in a small voice as he unzipped his pants, letting them fall to the floor. He was wearing his blue pair of briefs and she wondered if that had any significance.

He was staring down at her. "Are you going to get out of those clothes, or do I have to undress you?"

"You have to undress me," she said, loving the idea. But then he was dropping his briefs, and she realized that waiting for him to undress her would prolong things longer than she felt like prolonging them, so she quickly started taking off her clothes and tossing them on the floor.

"You look a lot more appealing than a prison guard," Richie said, his eyes caressing her naked body.

Phoebe pulled off the bedspread and got underneath the covers. "Umm, it's nice and warm under here," she told him.

"It's going to be warmer very shortly."

He got in the other side of the bed and pulled her close to him. "Going to prison this weekend was sure a good idea of yours. I didn't think we were ever going to get a chance to be alone."

"This wasn't what I had in mind."

"Not ever?"

"I mean I didn't have it in mind for this particular weekend."

"You've thought about it, though."

"Oh, yes. Haven't you?"

"All the time."

"Tell me what you thought about."

He propped himself up on one elbow and looked down at her. "Well, I thought about touching you like this," he said, his hand going to her breast. "And like this." There was a short pause while he found what he was looking for. "And most certainly like this." And then there was no further articulation of his thoughts, because he was kissing her, and caressing her, and what he was doing was more satisfying in every way than just talking about it.

WHEN HE WOKE UP it was light out and Phoebe was standing in front of the window. As though sensing his eyes on her, she turned around. "Her car is gone," she told him.

"Forget your sister," Richie said. "Has it stopped snowing?"

She nodded, not looking happy about it. "I suppose we'll have to leave," she said.

"Why should we have to leave?" he asked her. "You can have your mother bring Ben and Dory over here, I can build a few closets, you can paint the room white—"

She started to smile. "Don't forget the VCR."

"I was just about to mention it. So what do you think? Could you be happy spending the rest of your life living in a motel room with me?"

"You forgot the pantry."

"I'll start again," Richie said. "Could you be happy spending the rest of your life—"

"Yes."

"I haven't finished the question, Phoebe."

Her smile reached its anatomical limits. "What about Maggie?"

"Maggie? You want Maggie to live here with us, too? I suppose we could always adopt her."

"I mean, is it over with her?"

"It was over with her the first time I kissed you. I have one very bad failing, my love—I'm totally monogamous."

"I wouldn't call that a bad failing."

"Thank you for your vote of confidence. And if you'd like me to thank you in a more concrete manner, you could move that lovely body of yours back in bed."

"You haven't known me for a very long time, Richie."

"No, but I've been looking for you for a very long time." He lifted up the covers beside him. "Come on, Phoebe, this is Saturday. I think we can get away with staying in bed until noon."

She ran for the bed, sending it into a series of bounces as she dove under the covers. "This is too much fun to be real, Richie. I hope things don't change when we get back to Greensboro Bend."

"I expect lots of things will change."

"Do you?"

He nodded. "But for the better."

"There's something I think I ought to tell you."

"Oh, dear—true confessions time."

"I'm not using any birth control," she said, watching him for his reaction.

"I know that."

"How could you possibly know something like that?"

"Because, Phoebe, you're not the type to take birth control devices along when you visit a prison."

"Or anywhere."

"Right."

"So I could get pregnant."

"That's one of the possibilities, yes. The other is that you won't."

"But if I do?"

He drew her head down on his chest and stroked her hair. "I believe it was you who was feeling deprived last week because someone was having a baby and you weren't."

"Babies should have fathers."

"Sometimes you sound as innocent as Ben. All babies do have fathers, and we know who this one's father would be, don't we?"

"I'm talking about legal fathers."

"If you're going to go into a poor little unwed mother routine, Phoebe—"

"All I'm saying is—"

"Of course we'll get married. That goes without saying."

"It does not."

"Well, I just said it, didn't I?"

Phoebe took a deep breath, as though inhaling the happiness she was feeling. "Do you love me as much as I love you?"

"More. I love you two-thirds more."

"That's not possible," Phoebe said.

"You love Dory, you love Ben—"

"You don't love my children?"

He gave a greatly exaggerated sigh. "Let me say this just once, Phoebe, and listen closely. I love talking to you. I even love arguing with you. However, with two children—maybe three in nine months—the opportunities for us to be alone together are going to be rare. When they do occur, however, I don't think we should use them up by talking. Now we've got three more hours before it's back to the real world. Do you want to spend them arguing over who loves who more, or do you want to demonstrate that love in a more interesting way?"

She chuckled. "A more interesting way."

ONE THING LED TO ANOTHER and it was eight o'clock that night before they arrived at The Greenery to pick up the kids. Ben and Dory didn't seem overjoyed to see them, due in part to the quarters their grandmother had been giving them to feed the pinball machines.

"I was worried about you in that snowstorm," Katie Lou told them.

"We never made it to the prison," Phoebe told her.

Her mom scrutinized her thoroughly, then gave her a satisfied smile. "You're looking good, honey. Being sheriff seems to be good for you."

"It has its moments," Phoebe said, and saw that her mother appeared to know exactly what Phoebe was alluding to.

"I've put in a microwave oven," Katie Lou said. "You kids want to try one of my toasted cheese specials?"

Finding candy bars no substitute for real food, Richie and Phoebe didn't turn her down. They were sitting at the bar, wolfing them down, when a hush came over The Greenery. When Phoebe turned around to see what had caused it, she saw a familiar-looking man standing just inside the door.

"I don't believe it," Katie Lou gasped.

Richie did a double take and then a triple take, finally saying to the man, "Billy, is that you?"

His hair bleached a couple of shades lighter, his skin a healthy shade of bronze, his eyes clear, his step light, no doubt due to the vast reduction in the size of his gut, Billy approached the bar.

"So you did go fishing," Katie Lou said. "We were worried about you."

"You look great, Billy," Richie said.

"I didn't go fishing," Billy explained. "I went to a fat farm down in Florida."

"Well, I'm amazed," Katie Lou said. "You sure make all the other men here look like unhealthy specimens. Can I buy you a drink?"

"Gave it up, but I'll have some orange juice."

Ben came up to Richie and leaned against his legs. "Can we go over to your house, Richie, and watch a movie?"

"I didn't rent any, Ben. I thought we'd be away."

"Can we go over to your house and watch television?"

Richie looked over at Phoebe. "What do you think? You want to go over to my place and kind of sound the kids out about things?"

"I don't foresee any problems."

"Nor do I, but kids like to be let in on things."

"We like to be let in on watching television," Ben said.

"I CAN'T GET OVER Billy Benson," Phoebe said as they were driving home.

"I know. You think Katie Lou will view him differently now?"

"I have no idea. I'd also like to know what Mavis was up to."

"I'm sure there's a simple explanation."

"You two seem pretty happy," Dory said from the back seat.

There was silence for a few moments and then Phoebe said, "We are pretty happy."

"Is it something temporary, or is it something permanent?" Dory asked.

"What's a four-letter word for a state of permanent happiness?" Phoebe asked her.

"Love?" Dory asked.

"My daughter's a genius," Phoebe said to Richie.

"See, I told you," Dory was saying to Ben in the back seat.

"Yes," Ben said, "but I thought it was too good to be true."

Harlequin American Romance

COMING NEXT MONTH

#193 PLAYING FOR TIME by Barbara Bretton

Strange comings and goings, odd disappearances—Joanna's New York apartment building sizzled with intrigue. At the heart of it was Ryder O'Neal. She tried to maintain a safe distance from the elusive, mysterious man, but Joanna wasn't safe—from Ryder or from the adventure of a lifetime.

#194 ICE CRYSTALS by Pamela Browning

Monica Tye's entire life was focused on overseeing the training of her daughter, Stacie, as a championship skater, leaving her no time to sample the pleasures of Aspen. Duffy Copenhaver couldn't see the sense of it. Duffy had his own prescription for happiness—it included lots of love— but would the Tyes slow down enough to sample it?

#195 NO STRANGER by Stella Cameron

Nick Dorset dreamed of being in Abby's neighboring apartment. He longed to sit beside her, talk to her, hold her. But when she took off her bulky coat, Nick knew he would have to care for her, too. Abby Winston was pregnant.

#196 AN UNEXPECTED MAN by Jacqueline Diamond

When busy obstetrician Dr. Anne Eldridge hired handsome Jason Brant to cook her meals and clean her Irvine, California, home, she didn't dream that he would meddle in her social life. But Jason took it upon himself to protect Anne from her dismal choice in men. Was there a method in his madness?

HARLEQUIN HISTORICAL

Explore love with Harlequin in the Middle Ages, the Renaissance, in the Regency, the Victorian and other eras.

Relive within these books the endless ages of romance, set against authentic historical backgrounds. Two new historical love stories published each month.

Available now wherever paperback books are sold.

ATTRACTIVE, SPACE SAVING BOOK RACK

Display your most prized novels on this handsome and sturdy book rack. The hand-rubbed walnut finish will blend into your library decor with quiet elegance, providing a practical organizer for your favorite hard-or soft-covered books.

Only $9.95

Approximately 16" x 8" when assembled

Assembles in seconds!

To order, rush your name, address and zip code, along with a check or money order for $10.70* ($9.95 plus 75¢ postage and handling) payable to *Harlequin Reader Service*:

    Harlequin Reader Service
    Book Rack Offer
    901 Fuhrmann Blvd.
    P.O. Box 1325
    Buffalo, NY 14269-1325

    Offer not available in Canada.

*New York residents add appropriate sales tax.